ISSUE 3

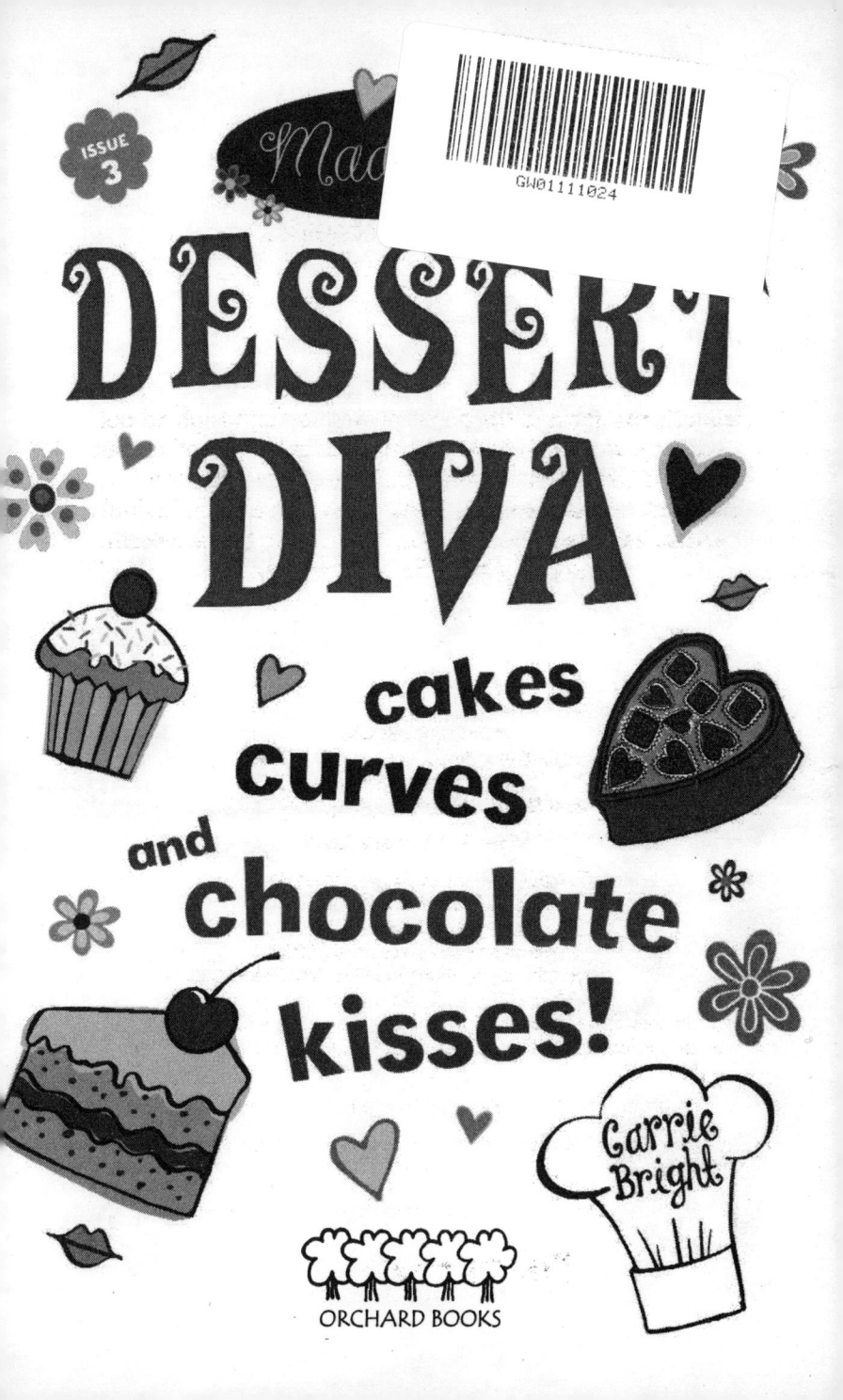

DESSERT DIVA

cakes
curves
and chocolate
kisses!

Carrie Bright

ORCHARD BOOKS

Hi, it's Maddy Blue here and I'm a total mag-hag - addicted to magazines!

When I'm feeling mad, sad or bad, I buy myself one, crawl between the bright, shiny pages and get lost forever. (Mad's note: Some people wish I would...)

So can they help me lose my sweet tooth...and resist the boy who's cooking up a recipe for romance?

Mmmmmmmmm!!!!

If my life was a magazine would it be a healthy number full of fitness tips and lite bites? Or a foodie title full of sweet treats and delicious desserts...?

You be the judge. Here's my life in a magazine. (Well kind of.)

Hope you enjoy it!

Maddy x

Maddy

The World's Top Teen Magazine!

written, edited, designed and published by

Maddy Blue

Issue No. 3:
Dessert Diva!

1. Eat yourself fit
2. Beat the bulge and still indulge
3. Is chocolate good for you?
4. Help – my sweet tooth's out of control!
5. Top three tips to avoid temptation
6. Rate your plate
7. Life is not a box of chocolates…
8. Eat humble pie
9. Good mood food
10. Make friends with food
11. Recipe for success
12. Just desserts
13. Passion cake
14. Feed your soul
15. Chocolate kisses
16. Eat cake and celebrate!

What's inside?

A MADDY BLUE PRODUCTION
Copyright © Maddy Blue Inc.

1

EAT YOURSELF FIT

> **EAT YOURSELF FIT**
>
> *The new magazine for girls who want to eat well...*
> *AND take the stress out of dropping a dress size!*
> *Too good to be true?*
> *Read on – the new fit and shapely you starts here...*

'Cake factory?' I stare at the screen in front of me. 'I'm going to work at Just Desserts – the *cake* factory? Pinch me – I'm in heaven!'

'It's not real work experience,' Scott points out. 'Don't get too excited.'

'Yes, but it's a taster day, and I'm going to sample every sweet in sight!'

(Mad's note: Just Desserts make cakes, desserts, puddings and sweet treats. Everything that is creamy, chocolatey and completely irresistible.)

We're in the Resource Centre at break checking out where we're going next week. It's a new idea to introduce us to 'the world of work'. The results have just been put on the school website so we can prepare ourselves.

'Congratulations – it's your dream job!' Starr laughs.

'Let's hope I get something as good.'

'Just don't overdo it,' Scott says. 'You're a real *Dessert Diva*. You've already worked your way through every pudding on the school menu – at least twice.'

'*Noooooo*, don't remind me! I was thinking about that only this morning. I've eaten so many puddings this winter I've turned into one. Too many humps, bumps and lardy lady lumps!'

'Hmm, so is this really a dream job?' Scott's got a point, but I'm one step ahead of him. He's so clever it's not often I can say that.

'Aha! I found a magazine to help me spring-clean my life. No more lumps and bumps – I'm going to eat myself fit. *Ta-daa!*'

I reach into my bag and pull out my new magazine. It's called *Eat Yourself Fit*. Perfect. Just reading the name makes me feel slimmer already. Who would have thought getting fit could be so easy?

'Maddy, you're fine the way you are. Chunky. Boys like that – trust me, I know.' Scott raises an eyebrow, trying to look super-cool.

If any other boy called me chunky I'd be hurt and offended, but Scott and I have been friends since nursery

– he's like a brother to me. So I punch him.

'Oi, what was that for?' he asks, rubbing his arm.

'I think you meant curvy,' Starr intervenes. 'An hourglass figure is very fashionable at the moment. Make the most of it, you're lucky.'

Starr is someone who eats all she wants and is naturally thin with supermodel looks. It's very annoying, but it's not her fault so I forgive her.

'Huh, if I've got an hourglass figure then all the sand has run to the bottom,' I sigh.

'You're not going to do anything stupid like getting into extreme dieting, are you?' Scott says, looking suddenly concerned – just like a best friend should.

'Course not, that's why I bought this mag.' I pass it to him and he flicks through the pages.

'*Eating yourself fit is about exercise and healthy eating*,' he reads aloud. 'I like it – this is my type of magazine!'

A healthy lifestyle helps you feel fit in both mind and body.
Get active, eat well and keep it fun!
Read on to find out how...

'Ooooh!' Starr squeals. 'Someone else is working at the cake factory too...' She taps my screen and I scroll down.

'*NATHANIEL TAYLOR,*' I read out loud. My face flushes the colour of strawberry jam, but I try to act casual. 'Oh, Fat Nat – fancy that. Well, at least it's someone I know.'

'Hang on a minute.' Scott turns to me. 'You just hit me for calling you *chunky* and now you're calling him *Fat Nat*! That's not right, is it?'

'But that's what he told us to call him!' I say, even though it does sound a bit wrong.

'Lovely Nat – he's got a bit of a thing for you, hasn't he?'

'No, Starr, I don't know what you mean.' I look back at the screen to hide my face. The problem with having good friends is that they know all your embarrassing secrets.

She's right. There is something simmering between us, but I'm still not sure exactly what it is.

(Mad's note: Taster day? Suddenly it looks like I've bitten off more than I can chew.)

'Anyway, where are you both working?' I say, hoping to change the subject.

'I'm going to a law firm.' Scott taps the screen. 'I asked for something either legal or scientific, so that'll suit me fine.'

'And I'm at Silver's, that designer clothes shop in town – yay!' Starr waves her arms around.

'Hmmm, your jobs are *sooo* grown-up. I'm starting to wonder if a cake factory is really *me*.'

'But a minute ago you said it was perfect!' Starr turns

to me in surprise. 'Was it the job you asked for? If not, you could complain.'

'Let's see...' I flick to my original onscreen application. 'Oh. *Er*...remember my Goth phase*?'

'How could we forget?' Scott groans. 'Love spells, black hair, black clothes, eyeliner...you even wanted me to wear guyliner. Ah, let me guess, you asked for a job in a crypt?'

'Almost...I wrote, *"Ideally I'd like a job in a funeral parlour. If that's not possible let Destiny decide."*'

'Well, you're lucky, then. A cake factory is definitely a more healthy option.'

'*Hmmm, s'pose.*' Now I'm confused and open my lunchbox for sweet consolation. 'Yuk. Nothing but a boring cheese sandwich. Anyone got any chocolate?'

'Are you sure chocolate is part of eating yourself fit?' Scott hands me a cereal bar. 'Try this instead.'

I read the label.

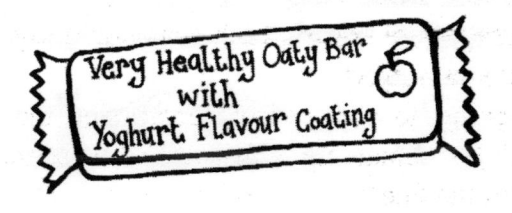

> Very Healthy Oaty Bar
> with
> Yoghurt Flavour Coating

'No thanks.' I pull a face and give it back. 'Did you know that "desserts" spells "stressed" backwards?'

(* Read all about Maddy's journey to the dark side in *Gothic Goddess*!)

'Fascinating.' Scott switches off his computer and stands up. 'But what has that got to do with anything?'

'Because it's what I am – *STRESSED*!' I'm worried about tomorrow already, and at times like this only chocolate will do.

2
BEAT THE BULGE AND
STILL INDULGE

> *Watching your diet doesn't mean denying yourself desserts — a sweet treat at the end of your meal.*
> *Common desserts include cakes, cookies, ice cream and fruits.*
> *We show you how to beat the bulge and still indulge!*

'Strawberry tarts.' Three girls and a red-faced boy step forwards. They're wearing white overalls and white hats, like me.

I'm at the cake factory, but ever since we put on the uniform it's like we're no longer human. I'm a chocolate muffin, apparently, and I notice that Nat is a frosted donut. Perhaps I'm dreaming.

'Swiss rolls, vanilla cupcakes, chocolate muffins,' someone shouts, and I step forwards.

Nat waves as I follow the other workers through the big swing doors at the end of the room to meet my *Cake-Fate*.

We march along a walkway overlooking acres of pink party sponges, mountains of multicoloured muffins and huge vats of chocolate and cream.

The smell is overpowering – sweet and addictive. This is confection perfection and suddenly I'm starving.

I could kill for a cupcake.

(Mad's note: A unique blend of cocoa, sugar, dried whey and unidentified emulsifying agents... Mmmmmmmmmmmmm!)

The rest of the morning blurs by in a frenzy of activity, and I discover that we're slaves to the conveyor belt. When it's switched on, hundreds of muffins come streaming towards us. We have to catch them and pack them into boxes to be sold in supermarkets everywhere.

It's torture, because the chocolate smells delicious and the muffins never stop coming! Wave after wave of them: white chocolate, choc and nut, double chocolate, triple chocolate – every variety of chocolate you can think of.

I get hungrier and hungrier, and then – just when I'm about to pass out – a loud siren sounds, the conveyor belt grinds to a halt and everything stops.

'Well done, love, you worked really well. You've earned your dinner,' a frilly-capped woman says to me as we march back up the steps.

'Thanks,' I say. 'Where do we—?'

'The staff canteen, just along there,' she points. 'And we get discount on all the desserts. That's one good thing about working here – you won't go hungry!'

Faster than it takes to say *chocolate chip cookie*, I go through the door and head straight for the dessert counter.

I'm dizzy with desire for desserts. After all, didn't I read that you can *Beat the Bulge and Still Indulge* in my mag this morning?

There was no time to read the whole page, but I got the general idea. Sweet treats are OK and right now there's work to do!

(Mad's note: So much to eat, so little time...)

My mouth starts watering as soon as I look at the menu...

Just Desserts

Today's Special: Death by chocolate cake

Baked to perfection, studded with chocolate chips, smothered with fudge topping and drizzled with white chocolate.

Even before I've finished reading, my hands are grabbing as many sweet treats as I can. And I don't even feel guilty, thanks to *Eat Yourself Fit*!

How To Beat The Bulge And Still Indulge...

1. Only take as much as you need. Sometimes a few bites of a rich dessert is just enough.

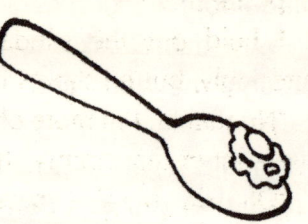

My tray is piled dangerously high with plates of cakes and sweet treats as I make my way through the crowded canteen. Then, when I lower it onto an empty table, my hands start shaking from sugar withdrawal. The strawberry sundae wobbles dangerously on the edge, and just as I reach out it topples over...

'Gotcha!'

A pair of hands shoots out and catches the long glass without losing a single strawberry or one blob of cream.

'Thank you!' I breathe with relief.

'My pleasure – it's so nice to see a girl with a healthy appetite.'

Nat smiles at me and my face heats up like an oven. Last time we spoke properly he asked me out and I gave him the 'let's just be good friends' routine. This is *sooo* embarrassing.

'I'm er...eating myself fit,' I explain. 'Lots of fresh fruit and *um*...cream.' I scoop a cream-covered strawberry off the sundae and pop it into my mouth.

(Mad's note: Mmmouthwatering – need I say more?)

'Would you like one?' I ask as he sits down opposite me.

I hold out the sundae and the strawberries shine enticingly, but he shakes his head.

'No thanks, I'm more of a fresh cream fan, myself. They use a lot of that squirty stuff here.'

'Oh, do they? I never really noticed,' I mumble between mouthfuls of sprinkles, ice cream and the odd piece of fruit. 'Why is it that things which are bad for you always taste so good?'

'Dunno. If you've got a sweet tooth you might like to try our Cake Bake at school tomorrow.'

'Mmm?' I try to ask a question but can't actually open my mouth as it's now crammed full of chocolate cake.

'We're cooking something special to sell at break-time. It's for Valentine's Day. Why don't you come by for a nibble?'

A cake crumb catches in my throat and sets me off coughing.

Nat gets up and smacks me on the back as I spray the tablecloth with half-digested cake crumbs.

'Sorry, that sounded so wrong. What I meant to say was that I hope you, Scott and Starr will drop by.'

I find my voice at last. 'OK, I'll let them know. So you like cooking?'

'A bit too much, unfortunately – as you can see.' Nat folds his arms, trying to hide his shape. 'But they do say never trust a thin chef, so I've found the perfect job. I've been doing a catering class for a while now and I'm loving it.'

'Hang on a minute – a few months ago you were into the Goth scene... So what do you cook? Roast bat in blood-clot sauce?' I pop another strawberry into my mouth.

'No, roast bat is *sooo* last season – and to be honest, I dropped out of the Goth scene when I took up cooking... Black was never really my colour,' he jokes. 'Now it's whites and a stripey apron.'

Just then the siren sounds and I forget everything in my extreme panic. There's still a *whole* caramel square sitting on my plate waiting to be eaten and we have to get back to the factory floor!

I take a big bite – and another, and another – savouring the rich chocolate, toffee and biscuit mixture. It's so creamy and buttery, just the way I like it – I'm in *Full-Fat Heaven*!

How To Beat The Bulge And Still Indulge...

2. Substitute key ingredients – such as cream and butter – with low-fat alternatives. Try natural yoghurt and low-fat spread. You'll never notice the difference!

'I hope you like my food as much as that,' Nat smiles. 'We're going to use fresh ingredients. Milk, butter, cream and eggs from local farms. I think it makes all the difference – wait and see!'

Nat waves his fork around enthusiastically and his dark eyes glow like melted chocolate.

Suddenly I'm seeing him in a whole new light.

He's sweet, he's funny and he likes cooking good food.

Hmm, shame he's not my type…

3

IS CHOCOLATE GOOD FOR YOU?

Chocolate is celebrated as 'Food for the Gods'.

But is it really good for you? Read on to find out if you should take care or take heart!

At the end of the day, I can't resist a visit to the Just Desserts discount shop. I feel sorry for all the misshapen cakes and chocolates with lumps and bumps in the wrong places. They remind me of me.

Nat appears as I queue up with a big bag of out-of-shape chocolate cakes. 'I promised a treat for my little brother, Max,' I explain, in case he thinks they're all for me. 'These will keep him going for ages.'

Take care...

Mass-market cakes and chocolates often contain high levels of sugar, artificial sweeteners and preservatives.

'Yes, this one lasts for...' – he examines the sell-by date on a chocolate brownie – 'a good six months, thanks to all the additives.'

'Really? That doesn't sound too healthy.' I hesitate at the checkout, wondering whether to put them back. 'I know my little brother is a pest sometimes – well, most of the time – but I don't want to poison him.'

'Don't worry, he'll survive,' Nat says. 'Just tell me what you think when you taste the real food tomorrow.'

Nat sits next to me on the bus home and I feel quite relaxed until it stops and starts in busy traffic. Then I start to deeply regret my cake intake at lunchtime.

(Mad's note: And the donuts and muffins at afternoon break!)

I close my eyes while Nat is talking, not because he's boring but because I start to feel sick. Very sick.

'And because you've got a sweet tooth I thought I'd have a go at making chocolate truffles,' I hear him say.

Take heart!

Handmade chocs can be more 'healthy' than shop-bought chocs.

Generally the darker the chocolate the better it can be for you.

'It shouldn't be too difficult. Melt some good quality chocolate, add fresh cream, maybe a few nuts and butter, mix it all up and—'

The bus lurches to a halt and my stomach lurches with it. I cover my mouth and mumble, '*Mgrrr*, my stop. Must get off!'

'Oh, OK. Nice talking to you, see you tomorrow!'

He waves as I stagger off the bus and it moves away. Then I sit in the bus shelter and wait for the waves of nausea to stop. At last I make my way home, feeling very sorry for myself...

'Food will be ready in five minutes!' Mum trills as soon as I walk through the door.

'Where's my treat? Where's my treat?' Max the human jumping bean leaps up at me, while Chester the dog sniffs my bags and barks excitedly.

'Leave me alone!' I wail, slumping down on the sofa

and covering my head with a cushion. 'I'm not well.'

Mum extracts the bags from my hand and takes out a misshapen muffin.

'Just one or you won't want to eat your meal,' she explains to Max. 'It's pasta, and I've made a lovely dessert for Maddy after her hard day at work. Chocolate mousse with—'

I groan, 'Stop talking about food! That's all I ever hear in this house! Food, food, food – there *is* more to life, you know.'

'Food! Foodie! Food! Foodie!' Max starts singing in a tuneless, pointless way, which gets louder and shriller with every word.

'Shut up!' I pull the cushion closer round my ears.

'Max, come and help me in the kitchen for a minute,' Mum says, in a voice as soothing as a cup of bedtime cocoa.

After a bit I haul myself upstairs and lie down on my bed. How do adults manage to go to work day after day after day? I've only done six hours and I'm *shattered*.

Chester, our old, smelly and overweight dog, hauls himself up beside me. I don't even have the energy to push him off so we snuggle down together and fall asleep.

'Tea's ready!' Mum calls a few minutes later.

I turn over and groan. My stomach aches and eating is the last thing I can do.

Finally she gets the message and brings me up a hot-water bottle and a glass of water.

After that I fall asleep again, only to dream of giant cakes rumbling towards me...

Next morning, the sun is shining and I wake up early after my long night's sleep, feeling much better.

Except that now I'm hungry.

There's a yawning chasm where my stomach once was, so I sneak down into the kitchen before anyone else is about.

I feel so good as I pour my semi-skimmed milk onto my healthy cereal and eat every mouthful slowly. It's only when I open the fridge to put the milk back that things start to go downhill.

It's when I catch sight of the bag of sweet treats I brought back for Max.

'*Eat me! Eat me! Eat me!*' they squeak.

Those poor little shapeless cakes are calling to me and I have to put them out of their misery.

'OK, just one!' I reply, because I can't bear to see them suffering.

(Mad's note: Talking to cakes - first sign of madness.)

I rustle around and find an out-of-shape cupcake. It's double chocolate with fudge frosting. *Mmmmm*, chocolate...

'No more.' I wag my finger at a broken-down brownie just begging to be taken care of...

But then the blood rushes to my face and there's a buzzing in my ears and I can't control my hand, which is reaching out for the brownie, and my fingers curl around it and –

'Good morning, Maddy. Have you had breakfast yet?'

Dad walks in and I shriek with shock as the sweet-treat spell is broken.

'No. Yes!' I drop the brownie like it's red hot. 'Gotta go. Byeee!'

When it's time to leave for school I risk coming back downstairs again, sighing and groaning. This time I'm armed with my magazine, which I've just read from cover to cover.

'Maddy, what is it, love?' Mum puts her hand on my shoulder and rubs my arm.

'Told you she was in a strange mood today,' Dad whispers, appearing behind her dressed for work. 'Hormones. You're best to deal with it, love,' he mutters, giving Mum a peck on the cheek and making his escape.

'I'm an idiot. I should have read it properly, from beginning to end!' I wail as the door shuts behind him.

Take care...
Chocolate and sweet things are a **TREAT** not a **TREATMENT**. Too much sugar is bad for you and can result in cravings and irritability.

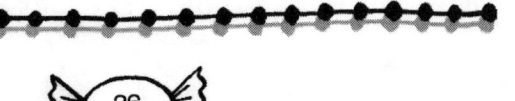

'What do you mean?' Mum looks mystified as I wave my mag at her.

'I thought I could eat myself fit and I got the wrong end of the stick. You have to educate yourself and learn about food and—'

'Now, Maddy, I hope you're not going to skip breakfast or anything silly like that?' She puts her hand on my forehead. 'You look a bit pale – perhaps you need something to settle your stomach. How about some toast?'

'Nooo!' I jump up and flounce out of the kitchen in a strop. 'Stop trying to force-feed me will you? You *always* do that!'

'Maddy, it's not force-feeding – it's a form of love.'

There's no answer to that so I resort to the blame game.

'Huh, now you're trying to make me feel guilty!' I shout downstairs. 'No wonder I'm upset – it's all *your* fault!'

4
HELP – MY SWEET TOOTH'S OUT OF CONTROL!

Eat Yourself Fit's Nutritional Advisor, Felicity Fitt, answers all your health and food problems. This week:

Help – my sweet tooth's out of control!

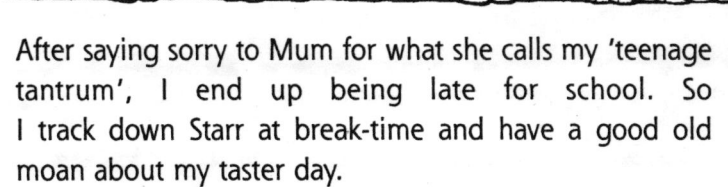

After saying sorry to Mum for what she calls my 'teenage tantrum', I end up being late for school. So I track down Starr at break-time and have a good old moan about my taster day.

'And according to this chart, at my weight I should be seven foot three!' I point to the pages of *Eat Yourself Fit* and Starr laughs.

'Don't exaggerate, Maddy. You're getting obsessed with all this stuff.'

'Am I? But honestly, Starr, working at that cake factory was a nightmare for me. It set me off on a serious sugar

DESSERT DIVA

spree. Then there were all these goodies to take home at knock-down prices—'

'Yes, I picked up a designer T-shirt for next to nothing – wait till you see it!'

We've reached our lockers now. 'Hmm, so you get new clothes and I get stale cakes! What work perks did Scott get, I wonder?'

'Do I hear my name spoken in vain?' Scott sneaks up and taps me on the shoulder.

'No, I was just asking about your taster day. What little freebies did you get at the law firm? Any gossip? The newspapers would pay a fortune for something juicy.'

Scott puts his fingers to his lips. 'Plenty, but I signed the Official Secrets Act, so if I tell you I'll have to kill you. Now, check this out for a proper taster day – right up your street.'

He passes me a leaflet.

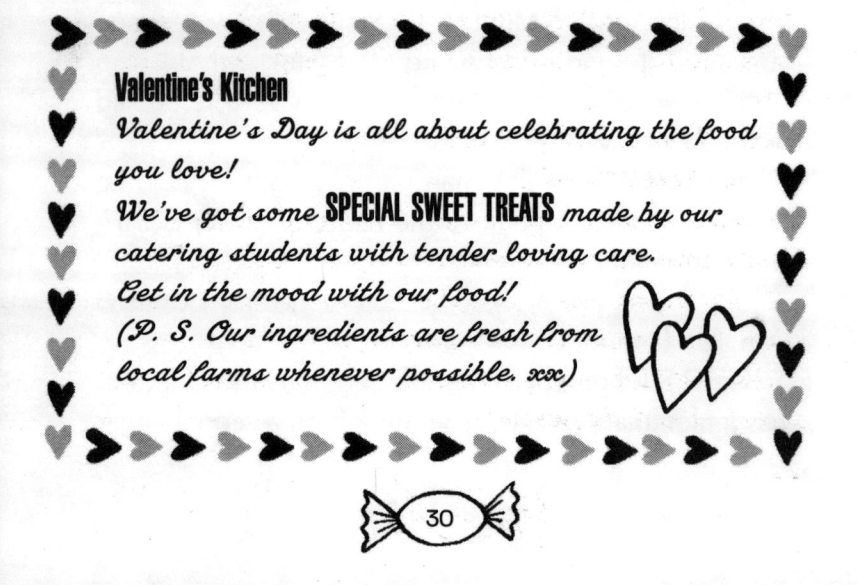

Valentine's Kitchen

Valentine's Day is all about celebrating the food you love!

We've got some **SPECIAL SWEET TREATS** *made by our catering students with tender loving care.*

Get in the mood with our food!

(P. S. Our ingredients are fresh from local farms whenever possible. xx)

'Oh, Nat told me about this yesterday – he asked if we'd all go!' I say eagerly, remembering Nat's enthusiasm and those chocolate-drop eyes...

'Even better! What are we waiting for?' Scott puts on his street voice. *'C'mon, dudes, let's head for the food!'*

Starr closes her locker and follows Scott, but I stay where I am. There's a terrible war raging in my body. My taste buds are tingling and telling me to move, but there's a voice in my head saying, *NO, NO, NO! Resist sweet treats!*

'You coming?' Starr calls over her shoulder.

'Um, just need to get something. See you there,' I wave back.

When they're gone I don't know what to do. I really want to support Nat, but I'm so weak-willed – how can I resist his handmade nibbles?

When in doubt whip your mag out – that's always been my motto. So I reach into my locker for the latest issue of *Eat Yourself Fit*, served fresh this morning.

Flicking through the pages, a letter leaps out at me.

Help – my sweet tooth's out of control!

Dear Felicity Fitt,

I need to get into shape, but my problem is that I can't resist chocolate and sweet stuff.

If my mum bakes a cake I can't stop at one slice. It's the same with sweets, and I love puddings, too – sometimes I skip savouries and just eat desserts.

Please give me some tips that will help me eat more healthily, because I'll never get into shape if I carry on like this!
Thanks!
Curvy Girl

I don't believe it – Curvy Girl is writing my life! Faster than you can say *Mississippi Mud Pie*, I devour the reply.

Dear Curvy Girl,
Everyone likes sweet treats now and again – but a balanced diet is best! For more help see my Top Three Tips to Avoid Temptation' on the next page.
As for being a curvy girl – there's nothing wrong with that! Make sure you exercise regularly to keep those curves in trim and looking good!
Wishing you health and happiness!
Felicity Fitt

Just as I thought – if I want to get in shape, I'll have to resist the temptation of Valentine's Kitchen.

Not only that – I'll have to resist Nat too.

(*Mad's note: I can resist anything...except temptation.*)

It makes me feel sad not to support him – he's such a nice guy – but it's no use.

He's my Nemesis.

He's Death by Chocolate.

I am a Dessert Diva and he's a Good Food Dude.

It's a bad mix.

5

TOP THREE TIPS TO AVOID TEMPTATION

TIP 1: FILLING FOODS
Eat plenty of fruit, veg and wholefoods such as pasta, potatoes, bread and rice. They fill you up so you don't crave sugary snacks.

So I spend my break-time crunching an apple and reading the *Top Three Tips to Avoid Temptation*. Then I take some exercise by walking round the schoolyard, watching the queue for the Valentine's Kitchen grow longer and longer...

'You missed out, girl – where were you?' Scott hisses at the start of our next lesson.

'Oh no! I started reading my mag and forgot all about it!'

'*Tcha!* Forgot? Are you mad? No magazine is better than good food.' Scott licks his lips and smiles at the memory.

'And Nat was asking where you were.' Starr looks at

me questioningly and I feel bad about my white lie, but how can I explain?

Scott and Starr are my best friends, but they wouldn't understand. They have a normal relationship with food. They can resist temptation, but I can't.

Only Curvy Girl and Felicity Fitt could understand a thing like that.

(Mad's note: Why can't I live in mag world instead of the real world? Life would be so much easier.)

Luckily our teacher launches into a 'SILENCE! IF YOU'VE GOT ANYTHING TO SAY THEN PLEASE SHARE IT WITH THE WHOLE CLASS' routine. This shuts us up for a while and saves me from any more awkward questions.

Scott has student council business at lunchtime, so Starr and I go off to the school café, where I am determined to stay on my healthy-eating track.

I opt for a wholesome baked potato with cottage cheese and salad, and try not to look at Starr's pizza and pudding option.

'So how are things at home?' I say when we sit down. This attempt at conversation is for two reasons:

a. Because I am genuinely concerned – Starr's chosen to live with her dad now her parents are getting divorced, but I don't think things are easy.
b. To divert the chat away from Nat and his romantic recipes.

'Oh, I forgot to tell you. Dad found a buyer for Bar Salsa. He says we can live with his parents until he finds somewhere smaller.'

'Is that good?' I ask, cutting up my lettuce and trying to ignore Starr's sticky toffee pudding – she's toying with it like its not worth eating.

(Mad's note: It's sticky, it's toffee and it's definitely worth a second helping!)

'Well, I love staying with my grandparents, so that's cool. And Dad's more of a musician than a businessman, so I'd say that selling Bar Salsa will be a weight off his mind. I just don't know how he's going to earn money, that's all.'

I push more greenery into my mouth to stop myself drooling and nod sympathetically. Starr sighs and pushes her picked-at pudding away. It's all I can do not to grab the bowl and lick it clean.

Poor Starr – whenever she's worried she can't eat. Unfortunately, whenever I'm worried I comfort eat. So I must be extra worried today, because that pudding looks absolutely irresistible.

(Mad's note: Well, perhaps with a bit more cream poured over it…?)

'Aren't you going to finish that?' I hear the words before I realise they're coming out of my mouth. How can I talk about food when Starr's fretting about her future?

Luckily there seems to be another reason for her food refusal. 'No, I'm not that hungry after the banana cake

I had at break-time. It was yummy – Nat made it himself. You missed out there, Maddy. Do you want to finish this?'

She passes the bowl towards me, and as the sticky sauce catches the light I swear it winks at me.

YES, YES, YES! I'm screaming inside. In my opinion no meal is complete without a sweet treat to finish it off.

I'm just reaching over for Starr's bowl when I remember *Eat Yourself Fit* and those Top Three Tips To Avoid Temptation.

TIP 2: KEEP HYDRATED
If you are still hungry at the end of a meal drink a glass of water.

'No, no, no. It looks horrible. Disgusting. Yuk. NO.' I push it away from me.

'Oh, OK.' She looks a bit surprised. 'Just asking.'

'Here, let me take it away for you.' I grab the pudding back. 'We need some water, anyway.'

I carry the bowl at arm's length, like it's going to explode, and slam it down on the returned-trays trolley. Then I pick up a water jug and bring it back to the table, filling our glasses to the brim.

Starr sips at hers while I start glugging it down as

though I've just spent six months in the desert.

Only when I look up – mid-glug – do I see Scott and Nat staring at me with strange expressions on their faces. What's going on? We don't usually sit with Nat at lunchtime.

I try to turn the glug into a ladylike sip, but it doesn't work, and I end up coughing and spluttering like an old drainpipe.

'*Cough* – hi – *splutter* – where did you two spring from?'

Scott sits down and grins, bashing me on the back in a big brother-type way. 'Nasty cough you've got there, Maddy. Maybe you should go to the doctor.'

I pump my purple face up and down, eyes popping out of my head, still wheezing.

Nat looks at me awkwardly, half-smiling, his dark eyes a mixture of sympathy and hilarity. I guess he wants to say hello, but doesn't want to look as if he's laughing at me. I waggle my fingers at him, trying to be friendly, and he smiles back.

'We've been cooking up an idea for the fundraising,' Scott says, looking very pleased with himself. 'So, Starr, is it OK if Nat joins us at your place tonight?'

Nat's smile slips and he shrugs. '*Erm*, I don't want to get in the way if you've all got plans already.'

'No – well, our plan was to talk about the fundraising, so that's perfect, isn't it, Maddy?'

I nod, finally getting the power of speech back. 'Yes, of course... Er, d'you want to sit down, Nat? Sorry

I couldn't get to your Valentine's Kitchen. I heard it went really well.'

He sits down, and while Scott and Starr are chatting away we grin at each other like idiots. I'm raiding my brain for something to say but my mental cupboard is bare.

'So, er... Nat—'

Luckily the bell goes and, for once, I'm glad to hear it.

'Oh – is that the time already? Must dash, I can't wait to get to Maths. Bye!' I sling my bag over my shoulder, give everyone a wave and make my way out of the café and across the schoolyard.

Of course, I'm so quick that the classroom is empty when I get there. Time for a mag-fest!

I reach down into my bag, but instead of glossy paper, my fingers curl around a box shape that I'm sure wasn't there before. I look around, but no one's coming, so I pull the mystery object out.

It's a red heart-shaped box tied with a satin ribbon – how romantic!

I hide it under the desk as a red flush creeps across my face. Nat must have put it there when he sat next to me. That's so sweet – but so confusing, too.

I can't resist a sneaky peek, so I gently untie the bow and lift the lid, balancing the box on my knees.

Ahhh. The sweet smell of chocolate and vanilla hits me full on. Breathing deeply, I drool at the most lush chocolate truffles I have ever seen in my life.

TOP THREE TIPS TO AVOID TEMPTATION

TIP 3: MAKE EATING FUN

If you have to buy sweets, then share them with your friends.

Of course, I could put the lid back on again...

Of course, I could wait and share them with Scott and Starr...

But it would be rude not to try just one, wouldn't it?

I lift a truffle to my lips, licking off some of the cocoa powder and icing sugar. Then I bite into it, savouring the sweet taste that lingers on my lips like a chocolate kiss.

Mmmmm-mmmmm.

After that there's no going back. The blood is pounding in my head and my ears are buzzing. People are coming into class now but that doesn't stop me sneaking the rest of them into my mouth one by one.

And each one is better than the last. When they're gone, my fingertips trawl the box to catch every last grain of sugar and cocoa.

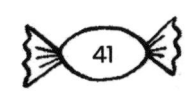

Consumed with passion.

Only when I look down desperately at the empty box do I see the handwritten words inside. And when I read them my heart starts pounding all over again.

Be my Valentine?

6

RATE YOUR PLATE

Rate your plate

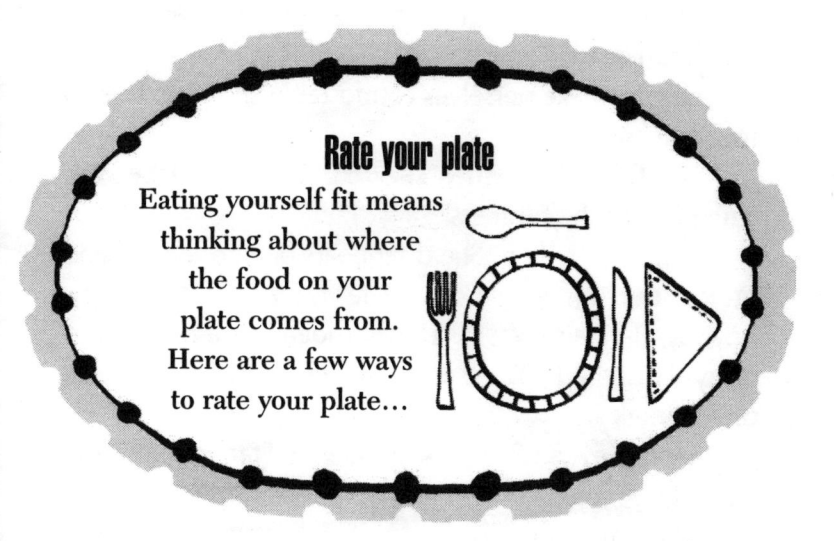

Eating yourself fit means thinking about where the food on your plate comes from. Here are a few ways to rate your plate…

'So, what are these plans you've been cooking up, then?' I say, careful to avoid looking directly at Nat. Neither of us has mentioned the mysterious Valentine chocs, but I'm sure he knows I've seen them by now.

The thing is, I just don't know what to say. Nat's not the one for me. I prefer mean and moody to cute and cuddly, but how can I explain that without hurting his feelings?

We're standing in the main room at Bar Salsa, which closed down yesterday, so everything is covered in white dustsheets. It looks sad and ghostly – a bit like Starr's dad, who haunts the other end of the room, strumming his guitar.

'Sit down, and make yourselves at home,' Starr says, pulling a dustsheet off two leather sofas and a low coffee table.

While we make ourselves comfortable she goes over to speak to her dad.

'Is he OK?' I ask when she returns. 'It can't be easy letting go of the business.'

'Yeah, he'll be fine.' She disappears behind the bar and brings out some glasses. 'The guitar's his therapy. Anyway, Bar Salsa was all Honey's idea. It's a bit big and glitzy for him – he wants to downsize. Some kind of small café, I think.'

'And Honey is…?' Nat whispers, as Starr pours water into a large jug.

'Her mum.' Scott fills him in. 'She lives in London now and they're getting divorced.'

'OK, right.'

We sit for a few minutes listening to the guitar music. It doesn't sound sad anymore, but relaxed and playful, like a cat chasing sunbeams.

Nat starts tapping out a rhythm on the arm of the sofa. 'This guy's got talent – his music's got *s-o-u-l*,' he says, stretching out the word.

I nod. I've always thought the same and can never

keep still when he's playing, either. Nat catches my eye and we both look away quickly.

'Sorry, it's only orange.' Starr brings the jug over. 'All the other soft drinks have been returned to the warehouse.'

'No worries.' Scott picks up his drink, takes a sip and leans back. 'Now for those fundraising plans. First, let me hand you over to my colleague, Mr Taylor. Tell us about your cakes, Nathaniel.'

'Thank you, Mr Lord.' Nat makes a mock bow. 'Let's see – there's lemon drizzle, apple and cinnamon, passion cake, chocolate cake—'

'Enough!' Scott says.

'No, don't stop – it's like poetry!' I breathe, gripping the sofa, my face growing suddenly hot. *Ooops – did I just say that?*

(Mad's note: *See? That sweet-talking is very addictive – it could be deadly!*)

'Yeah, I knew that would make you sit up and listen!' Scott laughs. 'And I still don't get why you weren't first in line at the Valentine's Kitchen today.'

Scott knows me far too well. I loosen my grip on the sofa and take a sip of my drink. I think I know where this is going, and it's not looking good.

'Um... All those cakes Nat listed. You're thinking of baking even more for the fundraising, are you?'

'Got it in one!' Scott reaches over to slap me a high-five, but I'm feeling far from happy. 'It was Nat who got me started on the idea – wait till you hear the story,' Scott continues.

'We've been doing a lot about where your ingredients come from on my catering course,' Nat explains, 'and trying to buy locally, so—'

'*Rate your plate!* I was just reading about that today!' I say, scrabbling around in my bag and pulling out *Eat Yourself Fit*.

(Mad's note: I do have a more-than-passing interest in food, which I'm happy to share.)

'Let's see... Here it is, look.' I give the magazine to Nat, who reads it out.

Rate your plate

Food grown locally can often be fresher, tastier and cheaper. Look out for free-range eggs from local farms.

'That's it in a nutshell – or eggshell,' Nat says, passing it back to me. 'We want people to think about what they're eating and where it comes from. So we have this big Cake Bake and—'

'We? We have to help make the cakes? But...I can't even boil an egg! And why cakes? Why not something less...you know, *tempting?*'

Scott tuts impatiently. '*Tcha!* You haven't even let us finish, Maddy... Then we got talking about other ingredients, like sugar, chocolate, banana, coffee – things you can't grow here.'

'And we've been learning about Fair Food projects as well. That's in this feature too, Maddy.' Nat points to the page and I skim the words.

Rate your plate

Look for special Fair Food labels on these foods:

Sugar   **Tea**   **Coffee**

Chocolate   **BANANAS**

It means that farmers have been paid a fair price for their crop. It tastes good – and you'll feel good, too!

'So we're going to raise money for farmers in places like Africa, Asia, South America and the Caribbean, as well as locally. Genius!' Scott finishes.

'But—'

'Wait up, there's more.' Scott raises his hand before I can carry on. 'This is where it gets *really* interesting. I did some research on the net, and they've even set up a farmers' co-op on St Lucia – back home!'

'Back home? Westfield's your home. You were born *here*, not the Caribbean!' It works both ways; I know Scott very well, too.

'Yeah, true, but one day I want to go back to visit with my mum, and *she* was born there. Wait till I tell her what we're doing. We've still got relatives on the island, y'know. It could help them directly!'

I can see that Scott is totally sold on this project. The more excited he gets the worse I feel. There's a growing hollow in the pit of my stomach – and for once it's not hunger.

'So what are you going to call the fundraising week?' Starr asks. 'We need a hook, don't we?'

'*Cake Bake Week?*' Scott says. 'How d'you think that sounds?'

'Boring. And selling cakes has really been done already. Can't we do something more healthy? A sponsored swim, perhaps?'

'No, this is the best idea yet. We already know the cakes sell well!' Scott sounds scandalised by my suggestion. 'What does everyone else think?'

Starr and Nat murmur their agreement and I know I'm on my own.

'OK, so all we need now is an idea for marketing it. That's where you come in, Maddy.'

'Me? But—'

'Yeah, you came up with brilliant slogans for the last fundraisers we did. You're right, though – Cake Bake is a bit boring compared to *Goth-Up and Cough-Up*.'

'And *More Dash Than Cash* from when we did the fashion show. That was a good one!' Starr agrees.

'So get your brain in gear. We want to sell food to raise funds for farmers at home and away. What shall we call it?'

The three of them are looking at me now and the pressure is on. All I can think of is the cake factory and that dream I had of those giant cakes rumbling towards me.

Of being out of control...

I glance at my mag for inspiration and it works. It makes me more determined that ever to fight the flab.

'*Eat Yourself Fit* is all about eating what's good for you.' I wave my mag in the air like a flag. 'And what are we going to do? We're telling everyone to stuff their faces with cake all week. It's all wrong.'

'No, it's not,' Scott explodes. 'This isn't about eating! It's about getting hardworking farmers a fair price for their food. Or the profits go to some fat cat middlemen!'

'But there must be another way!' The guitar stops and I realise I'm shouting now, but I have to make him understand. 'Lots of people are struggling with their weight these days and you're saying, *"Let's all eat cakes!"* What kind of message is that giving out?'

'Don't be such a drama queen! We're not exactly forcing people to eat, are we? You've got so obsessed since you bought that magazine. Lighten up!'

'I wish I could – that's the whole point. Some people are too heavy!'

'But it's good to have a sweet treat now and again, isn't it, Maddy?' Starr joins in.

'Yeah, fine for you – you can eat what you like and still stay slim! Some people only have to look at a cake and they balloon out. In fact... Yeah, I know, here's my slobby slogan for our cake-fest – *Eat Yourself Fat*!'

Nat looks down uncomfortably.

'Oh sorry, Nat, I—'

Of course that only makes things worse. I said the F word and I can't take it back. He might call himself Fat Nat, but coming from me it sounds like an insult.

The silence goes on forever.

I bite my lip and close my eyes – if only I could eat my words and start again.

'So let's put it to the vote then, shall we?' Scott's deep-freeze voice tells me exactly what he thinks of my opinions. 'Who votes for the Cake Bake?'

I look at Starr, who gives me a weak smile. For a moment I think she understands. Then she puts her hand in the air. Scott does the same but Nat is still looking at the floor, as if he wishes he were somewhere else.

'Nat?'

At the sound of Scott's voice he slowly raises his hand, without looking at anyone.

'So that's sorted then,' Scott says. 'Cakes it is. Maddy, are you with us?'

Hot tears are pricking my eyes and I'm using all my energy to fight them back. I shake my head.

'No. Sorry, I just can't do it.'

As soon as I say it I know that things have changed. They're my friends, but I don't I belong here anymore.

So I do the walk of shame over to the door. My footsteps echo on the polished wooden floor and no one tries to stop me.

7

LIFE IS NOT A BOX OF CHOCOLATES...

> *Life is not always sweet and full of nice surprises.*
>
> Here are some ideas for how to cope when things turn bad...

So I rush home, run upstairs and throw myself on my bed. How do I feel? Sad? Tearful? Angry?

No.

I feel hungry.

Like there's a huge hollow in my stomach, and no matter how much chocolate I eat, nothing will fill it.

Why can't I *think* before I open my mouth?

(Mad's note: That goes for words as well as food.)

I've just trashed Scott's idea, insulted Nat *and* moaned about my life, when Starr's got more than enough on her plate already.

I bet they all hate me. Even *I* hate me.

I need chocolate or cake – anything sweet and sinful that has nothing to do with real hunger and everything to do with the fear of losing my friends.

I'm pressing my fist into my mouth and crying dry tears of agony now. Eating's only going to make me feel even worse, and I know it, but there's a buzzing in my head and it's drowning out the voice of reason.

When in doubt – whip your mag out. That's my other life-saver. I'm a self-confessed mag-hag as well as a Dessert Diva. Ideally I'd be reading my mag while dipping into dessert, but luckily my bedroom is a cake-free zone.

I flick through the glossy pages and – as if by magic – words leap out that could have been written just for me.

Stress busters!

Don't reach for chocolate, cakes or cookies when you're stressed. Remember – a moment on the lips is a lifetime on the hips.

Get moving instead, and you'll feel and look a whole lot better.

Try dancing, walking, jogging or swimming.

So I put on some music louder than loud and dance. Extreme bedroom-type dancing – lip-pouting, hip-wiggling, shimmying, disco-posing moves that should never, ever be seen in public.

'Maddy! Maddy! What you doing?' Max is banging on the door, and it's only when I collapse back onto the bed for a breather that I hear him.

For once...I'm quite glad he's around. I've just read that it's easier to keep up an exercise plan with a friend.

(Mad's note: OK, so a four-year-old brat of a brother might not be technically classed as a friend, but I don't exactly have too many choices.)

'Come in, Max. D'you want to dance to the music?'

'Maxi dance! Maxi dance!' he chants, hurtling in, followed by Chester the wheezy dog. For the next few minutes we have a disco – which then turns into jumping on the bed – and conga-ing down the stairs. Of course, as soon as I go near the kitchen, Mum offers me a piece of the apple pie she just baked. Typical! Then I get even more of a workout running back up the stairs.

Later on I have soup and a sandwich in my room and fall asleep reading a pile of my magazines.

When I wake up the next morning, every cheerful cliché I ever read in my mags pops into my brain.

✳ Today is the first day of the rest of your healthy-eating life!

✳ **Every healthy-eating journey starts with one small bite!**

✳ **One size fits all! (Oops, that's a lie and popped in from nowhere...)**

The sun is shining and I'm determined to keep busy and take my mind off the mess I've made of my life.

Unfortunately my new best friend, Max, has a birthday party to go to today. Luckily my other new best friend – the dog – could do with a walk, so I volunteer to take him to the park.

Chester waddles along beside me, creaking and wheezing from old age and excess weight. Walking so slowly gives me a chance to think about the consequences of what happened yesterday, and it's not good.

What's going to happen when I see Scott and Starr again at school on Monday? They seem to think I'm stressing and obsessing about food – as well as being selfish and shallow. It's going to be very hard not to live up to that impression, but they're wrong. I do think fundraising for Fair Food is a great idea and I would love to help somehow. But by doing what?

As for Nat – I feel so guilty about using the F word on him, especially after his sweet present of those gorgeous chocs. He looked so down when I left – like a deflated soufflé. Somehow I have to make it up to him, too.

After ten minutes' strolling around a few daffodil beds in the park, Chester's gasping for breath. Well, I am too, so we find a sunny spot and I sit down on a wooden bench eager to catch some rays. I'm just closing my eyes when...

'Hi Maddy! Don't see you here very often – what's going on?'

I open my eyes and am surprised to see Zac – the sportiest guy in our year. He's dressed in shorts, T-shirt and trainers, even though there's a chill in the spring air, and he's jogging on the spot.

Zac doesn't even know I exist at school so it's a bit of a shock to have his full attention. He's good looking in a fashion-catalogue sort of way and is usually surrounded by giggling girly girls.

'Oh, I'm just taking the dog for a walk – getting fit, you know,' I say casually.

'Yeah?' he bounces onto the bench and sits right next to me. Then he stretches his arm across the back – giving me a panoramic view of his armpit. A pungent smell of *Essence de Sweat* hits me full on.

'Just beat my personal best. Took 4.8 minutes to run here from my house,' he says, twiddling a few knobs on a watch that's built like a spaceship.

'Congratulations! I made it from home to the park in the record time of...ooh, about 3 hours 20.'

'Good for you,' he says as the joke soars over his head.

'You know, if you got in shape you might be quite fanciable.' He sleazes a bit closer and there's that unmistakable whiff again.

I shrink back. 'Well, actually this walk was just a warm up. I'm on a complete exercise and healthy-eating kick at the moment.'

'Now you're talking! I just got A-plus for my unit on sports nutrition. Anything you want to know about healthy eating, Zac's your man!'

'You are?' I perk up a bit at this. After all the stick I got from Scott it's good to find someone who knows what I'm talking about.

'Yeah, protein shakes, carbohydrates, calcium intake, you name it...'

'Hmm, doesn't sound very appetising,' I say, remembering Nat and his poetic menu of cakes.

'Why should it? Food is just body fuel, after all. Wouldn't it be great if we didn't have to waste time cooking and eating? If we could just swallow a pill and a chemical drink every day?'

'Yuk, don't like the sound of that! Wouldn't you miss chocolate?' I ask, licking my lips at the memory of Nat's chocolate kisses.

'No – *eat to live*, that's my motto.'

'And don't we all eat to live?'

'Some people *live to eat*. Think about it.' He taps his head. 'Sounds like you're one of them. Start thinking of food as body fuel. More time for workouts. Feel that.'

He thrusts his arm under my chin and the smell of

stale sweat hits me full on. I stop breathing. 'Sozzy?'

He flexes a bicep. 'There, see? I know just what to eat and how to exercise so my body is sculpted. Wanna see my six pack?'

'No, no, keep your flapjack, er, flatpack covered up, thanks,' I say, getting hot and bothered. 'Come on, Chester. Time to go!'

I tug the dog's lead hopefully, waking him up. He yawns and eyes me sleepily, then lies down again.

'I've got calf muscles like concrete,' Zac says, stretching out his legs.

'Lovely! Sorry – Chester's desperate for a walk!' I say, nudging the dog with my foot so he finally stands up.

'What about my gluteus maximus – *it's rock solid*!'

'Bye now!' I pick Chester up – he's also rock solid – and stagger away with him in my arms.

(Mad's note: Dog carrying – very good for building your biceps.)

8
EAT HUMBLE PIE

> **Test your knowledge of foodie phrases with our fun and cheesy quiz!**
>
> Choose (**a**) or (**b**) and check your answers at the end.
> **1.** Cheesed off – what does it mean?
> (**a**) Miserable, fed-up, depressed.
> (**b**) Chased off by something yellow and smelly.

I keep checking my phone in the hope that it's broken.

It's not.

The reason it hasn't made any noise is because none of my friends have called me.

Or the reason could be because I don't have any friends.

If only I could eat my words, or eat humble pie – or eat anything that would make it all right again. But for once, I've lost my appetite, and if I called them I wouldn't know what to say.

> **2.** Eat your words – what does it mean?
> **(a)** You've said something stupid and wish you could unsay it.
> **(b)** You're eating a bowl of alphabetti spaghetti.

After lazing around in bed all morning reading and rereading copies of *Eat Yourself Fit*, I finally get up and head downstairs for a healthy breakfast.

OK, so I'm not exactly jumping for joy when I've eaten it, but at least I no longer want to crawl back into bed and hide from the world.

There's nothing else to do so I might as well try some exercise again.

Jogging is off the list for fear of bumping into Flat-Pack Zac, but my mag has given me another idea – swimming.

The last time I went to a swimming pool was weekly lessons at primary school, so I'm not looking forward to wearing my moth-eaten swimming cozzie in public. But if I don't go, what else is there to do? Nothing, except sitting around the house all day, torturing myself with dreams of desserts...

I think of the new fit and healthy me and start fishing around in my drawers.

'What you doing?' Max wanders in just as I find my cozzie and bundle it into a towel. Seeing him gives me an idea. If he comes too I can pretend to give him lessons and won't look like such a Maddy no-mates.

'Going swimming, Maxi – d'you want to come with me?'

He shakes his head. 'No, Maxi got football. *Boof!*' He kicks an invisible ball then runs off with his hands in the air, shouting, '*Goooooooooaal!*'

How could I forget? He's been going on about the match of the century all week. It's his team – the Tiny Tearaways *vs.* Dynamo Sunbeams.

I sigh – that boy has a better social life than I have.

At the pool I check the times. It's only open for another hour, so I hope it'll be almost empty. Most normal people will be back home getting ready for a long, lingering Sunday dinner…

Argh! I'm doing it again. There must be more to life than food – or thinking about food.

I plan my exercise workout and decide to do ten minutes in the pool – after all, *Keep Yourself Fit* says you mustn't overdo things at first.

In the changing room I hit my first problem – my swimming cozzie must have shrunk in the wash!

I wriggle and squeeze myself into it, trying to stretch it to cover my embarrassment. There's no mirror in the cubicle, but when I step out to find a locker a horrific sight meets my eyes.

Aaargh! I look like a monster from the deep! The tiny scrap of Lycra shows off every hump, bump and lardy lady lump to perfection.

What I need is one of those Victorian bathing machines pulled by a horse to the edge of the pool. Then I could walk down the steps in my frilly, woolly, figure-hiding knickerbockers, and no one would ever know what was underneath.

Sadly, that isn't an option. So instead I slope out wrapped in a towel – then drop it and dash down the steps, splashing about in shock as the cold water hits me. I kick off from the side and stretch out my arms in the water, resigned to my cold, watery fate...

And once the numbness wears off and the feeling returns to my limbs, I actually start to enjoy it!

Stretch pull, stretch pull – my body falls into a rhythm and my arms, my legs, my whole body relaxes.

Aaahhh! My mind clears of cakes, curves and carbs. It's just me, the water and the other swimmers.

Except... There's something very familiar about the figure in front me.

Isn't it...?

No.

It can't be, can it?

Yes it is.

Nat is bobbing towards me at an alarming rate and I really don't want to be seen like this.

In a panic I dive underwater and pass by him in a blur, pumping back up the pool as fast as I can. The plan is to keep in front of him so he doesn't see me. When he's safely at the other end I stand up, look down, and then dive back underwater again.

Nooooo! My swimming costume is so old and worn that it's not only tight, but see-through when wet. Now I'll have to stay in the pool until every single person gets out.

One by one all the swimmers disappear.

All except Nat.

I'm getting wrinkly as a walnut from staying in so long. Not only that – I'm exhausted at keeping as far in front of him as I can.

Can't go on! Must rest! Think I'm going to sink! My arms and legs feel like jelly, but I manage to grab the side-rail and hang on, panting and wheezing, feeling anything but fit.

'Maddy, is that you?' Nat swims up to me and catches the side of the pool too. Now we must look like a couple of seals bobbing around in the water, chatting about the price of fish.

'Oh – *puff!* – Nat! I didn't see you – *wheeze!* – What a surprise!' I'm so relieved he's actually talking to me that I start waving my arms around and nearly drown in the process.

'Pool's closing! Everybody out!' an attendant shouts as I surface.

'Oh, er, ladies first.' Nat nods towards the steps.

'No, no, you're nearer. You go first.' I bob up and down, trying to tread water and swim backwards away from the steps.

'One minute left – clear the pool, please!' The attendant glares at us.

DESSERT DIVA

'To tell you the truth, Maddy, I came here to get in shape, but it hasn't worked yet. I'd rather you didn't see me when I got out of the pool, so—'

---

3. Eat humble pie – what does it mean?
(a) Say sorry, apologise.
(b) Sample the latest celebrity chef's creation.

'Oh dear, I hope it isn't because of what I said the other day. I feel awful about that. I'm so sorry,' I say, forgetting to move my legs and swallowing a mouthful of water as I sink.

'Don't worry. Listen, let's have a chat when we're out of here,' Nat says. 'You can give me some swimming tips. I can't believe how fast you were, powering up and down the pool.'

'Well...yes, I was quite motivated.'

'Really, what's the secret?'

'Um, well, I didn't want you to see me in my swimming costume when I got out, either. It's see-through and I don't want to, er...show off my cupcakes.'

Nat lets out a snort of laughter, which turns into bubbles as he disappears underwater.

'Quick, the attendant's coming back,' I say, as he marches towards us from the other end.

'See you outside. Do you think you could look the other way now, please?'

I close my eyes. There's the sound of splashing, and when I open them again he's gone.

Foodie phrases quiz answers

Mostly (**a**)s – top marks for foodie phrases!
Mostly (**b**)s – you've got egg on your face!

9

GOOD MOOD FOOD

Lift your mood and boost your energy by eating the right food!

We show you how...

'You hungry?' Nat asks when I emerge from the changing rooms, looking wet and bedraggled.

'Starving,' I admit. It seems a long time since breakfast and I didn't mean to stay in the water for so long.

Even though the pool is closed, the Sports Centre is still open for another hour. We wander over to a soulless eating area with plastic tables and vending machines.

'So much for swimming and getting fit.' I stare at their bright rows of snacks and sweets, feeling dizzy and shaky.

'I know I shouldn't, but I'm desperate for a sugar rush!' I fumble around for some coins to feed the machine, hating myself all the while.

'Hold it right there, Miss *Eat Yourself Fit*!' Nat says in a comedy cartoon voice. 'Is it a bird? Is it a plane? No, it's Fat Nat – Super Chef to the rescue! *Ta-daa!*' he chants.

I turn my head to see him pull a large metal flask out of his backpack.

'What is it?' I ask. 'Unlimited coffee?'

'Nope, this is Standby Soup – locally grown veggies of course. Made by my very own hands. D'you want some?'

'Mmm, please. It sounds er…different,' I say, feeling secretly disappointed. I don't want to hurt him, but how can soup possibly compare to sweets?

He pours out the steaming soup into a plastic cup and passes it to me.

'It's the first time I've tried this recipe, so I hope you like it,' he says, suddenly less confident.

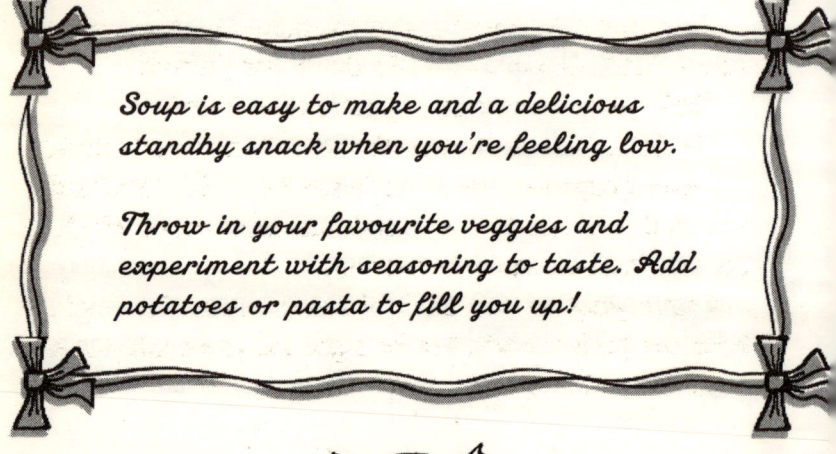

Soup is easy to make and a delicious standby snack when you're feeling low.

Throw in your favourite veggies and experiment with seasoning to taste. Add potatoes or pasta to fill you up!

I breathe in the warm, comforting aroma – it smells wholesome and herby. When I sip it down, I feel like one of those adverts where a warm red glow lights up your body from the top of your head to the tips of your toes.

'Mmm, this is delicious!' I say, and this time I mean it.

Nat smiles and pours a cup for himself. We sip in comfortable silence.

(Mad's note: Apart from the odd sluuurpp.)

After my soup I feel strong enough to speak the words I've wanted to say for days.

'Nat, I'm sorry about...you know, the other day, that argument? Well, I didn't mean to offend you by...'

I trail off, not sure what to say next. This started as an apology, but I've got a sinking feeling it will make things worse. I try again.

'Well, you know, it might have sounded as if I was calling you...*um*...'

'Fat?' Nat puts me out of my misery. 'But that's who I am – Fat Nat!' he laughs. 'So don't worry about it.'

'Well, yeah. I s'pose so. If you're OK with it?'

He sighs. 'Not really, but it's me, isn't it? I don't think I'm ever going to have a movie-star bod with rock-hard abs and a six-pack.' He stands up and poses which, considering his size, looks hilarious.

I start giggling and think of Flat-Pack Zac. He might have the perfect body, but he's got the personality of a piece of furniture.

'You know, you really got me thinking the other day.' Nat collects my empty soup cup and starts to tidy things away. 'What you said sounded a bit harsh, but it made sense too. I want to study all there is to know about food and you made me curious. So I even bought this...'

Good food = good mood

Simple and delicious!

Try...
Standby Soup
Serves 2
Use local veg for extra goodness!

1 carrot
1 leek
1 stick of celery
1 courgette
1 onion
1 clove of garlic
  (peeled and crushed)
1 tomato

He opens his backpack and pulls out a copy of *Eat Yourself Fit*.

'Omigod, I can't believe you bought that! Why?'

'You've just eaten one of the reasons. It's got great recipes for Good Mood Food this week.'

---

1 tbsp oil
stock (1 or 2 stock cubes in 1 pint/600 ml water)
1 tbsp frozen peas
1 tbsp small pasta shapes
$\frac{1}{2}$ tsp dried mixed herbs
1 tbsp tomato paste
salt and pepper

Wash, peel and chop all the veggies. Heat the oil in a saucepan and throw in the onion, carrot, leek, celery, courgette and garlic. Cook gently for 5 minutes. Add the stock, herbs, salt and pepper. Bring to the boil, then lower the heat and simmer for 20 mins. Add the tomato, peas, pasta shapes and tomato paste. Cook for another 10 mins.

Enjoy!

'Has it? Think I skipped those – I'm hopeless in the kitchen. More of a looker than a cooker.'

'Oh no, everyone can cook. Honest – there's nothing to it. That soup was child's play. I could show you if—' Nat shrugs and looks a bit unsure of himself.

I'm not surprised. He gave me those Valentine's chocs and I didn't say a word about it. He must wonder what's going on. Well, I'm not sure myself, but at least we can be friends again.

I smile at him, pleased that there's at least one person on this planet who doesn't hate me any more. At least, I don't think so.

'You know, it does say in here that it's easier to keep fit with an exercise partner...' I begin.

'Yes?'

'So, I, er, wondered if we could do a swap. You could be my foodie buddy and I'll be your exercise buddy. You know, swap some good food recipes for some time swimming and walking, and—'

'Exercise buddies? Yes, I'd like that. As long as it doesn't involve any jogging or skin-tight Lycra.'

'Definitely not! So, will you teach me how to cook some Good Mood Food?'

'Deal. If you keep me company on the long, hard road to getting fit.'

We shake on it.

'So, I'll see you in the kitchen at lunchtime tomorrow, then?' Nat says after we pack up our things and prepare to go our separate ways. 'Your first cookery lesson.'

'*Um*, well, I'm not sure. Oh, not that I've changed my mind!' I can see the confusion on his face and blurt out, 'Will Scott and Starr be there?'

'Yes, we planned to start cooking for Cake Bake Week.'

'Oh, right. Time for another piece of humble pie and, er...there's something else.'

'Uh-huh?'

'Well, I've got a bit of a thing about cakes, desserts – *anything* sweet! If I'm not careful I'll be licking out the mixing bowls and sneaking free samples and—'

'Tell me about it – how d'you think I got to this size?'

'Well, d'you think we can help each other to resist? I don't really want everyone to know my sweet tooth secret – it's embarrassing!'

'OK, we'll think of something. And I bet Scott and Starr will be cool with you. They're your friends, aren't they?'

'After Friday I don't know any more.'

'Well, it might take a day or two. I mean, they just want to sell some cakes to raise money for Fair Food, but you... You looked at it differently and thought of another angle. That's not selfish, that's...'

'Annoying?'

'No, it's um...unusual. Unique. It got me thinking, anyway. That's why I bought your magazine and ended up in the swimming pool.'

'Really? Thanks.'

Suddenly I feel a whole lot better and it's all thanks to Nat. At least he doesn't think I'm totally mad.

'You know, I would like to help Scott and Starr, and I do believe in Fair Food. But I wasn't lying when I said the Cake Bake was a bit boring. I know it could be bigger and better.'

'OK – I believe you. What did you have in mind? Some amazing, fantastic, mind-blowing idea? Tell me all.' Nat looks at me, his face glowing.

'I...*erm*...well, nothing yet – I just know we can do more. Sorry, sometimes my mouth just runs away with me. Food, words, it happens all the time.'

Nat opens his mouth like a fish, grilled on its last gasp. 'Ah.'

10

MAKE FRIENDS WITH FOOD

Make friends with food

Learn to cook some basic dishes – it's creative and fun, too.

Invite your friends over to share the results...

Scott doesn't call for me to walk to school on Monday morning. Not that I expected him to, but it still hurts. Even when we were at nursery we'd walk there with our mums. Then when we got older it was just the two of us.

Now it's me, myself and I.

He must be really upset not to call round.

Somehow, Scott and Starr avoid me all morning – or I avoid them. It's difficult to tell because I keep my head down and don't even look their way. That's going to change now, though, because it's lunchtime and I'm heading to the Cookery Department.

I stop and take a deep breath before pushing the door open. Now I know what a lobster feels like before it's plunged into boiling water.

'Hi,' I squeak as I walk in. 'Wondered if you needed any help with the cakes?'

Nat turns around. He's dressed in a stripy apron and stands in front of a mixing bowl. 'Maddy! Good – the more the merrier. I'll just get you an apron and then fill you in on the game-plan.'

Meanwhile, Scott and Starr stare at me like I'm the last stale cake on a plate.

'Um, s-sorry about the other day,' I say, tracing a line through some spilled flour on the work surface. 'D'you think we can bury the hatchet – and not in my head?'

Starr laughs.

'You really serious about helping?' Scott says, still not looking like his old self just yet.

I nod. 'I've never baked a cake in my life, but if Nat can give me some tips, I'll have a go.'

'Yes, it's my first cake, too.' Starr seems friendly already, but she stays next to Scott and I'm still not sure if he's forgiven me.

'We thought we'd have a go at making a few simple recipes today – just to see how hard it is. Then we can plan a cookery countdown to Cake Bake Week,' he says.

'And how long have we got until the Great Cake Bake?' I try to sound brief and businesslike to show Scott I'm serious. So it's a surprise to see him smile.

'*The Great Cake Bake*. Yes, that's got a ring to it.

Mind if we use that phrase? It's not trademarked to Maddy Blue?'

'Yep, it's an exclusive Maddy Blue™, but to a friend it's free.'

Scott hesitates, and before he can answer Nat appears with an apron.

'I've put you on grater duty,' he winks. 'Apples, because – surprise! – we're making an apple cake. You OK with that?'

'Very grate-ful, ha!' I joke, but secretly I'm pleased. Nat's trying to keep me away from anything too tempting.

'Scott and Starr have the chocolate cake to do and they're already *mise en place* – so you can get going, guys.'

'Yes, chef!' they say, saluting.

'Miz on plaz? What does that mean?' I ask, lifting the apron over my head and fastening the ties at the back.

'It's French for "everything in place". For a kitchen to run smoothly, it's best to go through the recipe and prep all the ingredients before you start.' Nat puts the apples and a grater in front of me.

'Prep?' I say. It's really weird hearing Nat spout all these strange words, but it puts me in awe of him a bit too. There's a whole world of food and cooking out there that I know nothing about.

'Prep – prepare by measuring out or chopping up or whatever. Just run through the ingredients, will you?'

Nat puts a folded-up page in front of me and I read aloud...

Nat's easy apple cake

2 large cooking apples
(locally grown)

250g margarine
(cut into cubes)

450g self-raising flour

225g granulated sugar
(Fair Food)

150g dried mixed fruit
(Fair Food)

4 eggs (from
local chickens)

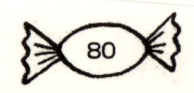

'Did you write this?' I ask.

He nods. 'Yep, adapted from a recipe in *Eat Yourself Fit*. Remember those Good Mood Foods? This cake has one of your five portions of fruit or veg a day—'

'Yeah, but it's still cake and I'm still a Dessert Diva – I can't resist,' I whisper. 'Don't let me near it, because I can't be responsible for my mouth actions!'

'Don't worry. That's why you're on grater duty. I have *grate* expectations of you, Maddy.'

I give him a look.

'So, can you get on with that while I weigh out the rest of the ingredients?'

I glance over to where Scott and Starr are sorting out stuff for the chocolate cake. That's when I spy a bar of Fair Food chocolate just loitering on the work surface. How can they ignore it like that?

(Mad's note: It's loitering with intent...to be eaten by me!)

I turn my back on it and take a deep breath. Focus.

'Er, do I need to peel this fruity thing first?'

'Nope, just grate it, skin and all, right down to the core. It's all good.'

'Right.' I grasp it in one hand and have a go. Finally, I end up with a soggy bowl of grated apple, which is rapidly turning brown.

'Is this what's supposed to happen?' I peer into the bowl suspiciously.

'Yep.' Nat hardly glances at it. 'OK, we're *mise en place* good. Now for the fun bit.'

I stare at the bits and pieces he's put out on the

worktop. Bowls of flour, sugar, raisins, eggs. Who could imagine they'd actually turn into a cake? It's like magic.

'So what now?'

'Now you have to get your hands dirty. Oh – you did wash them first, didn't you?'

'Of course – what a question! So, why do I get them dirty?'

'Look and learn, my foody buddy.' Nat tips the cubes of margarine into the bowl of flour, then plunges his hands into it.

'The idea is to rub the fat into the flour till you get the texture of breadcrumbs,' he says, sounding exactly like a TV chef.

'OK, here goes.' It feels like I'm back at nursery doing 'sand play', but I soon get the hang of it and it's fun.

Looking across at Starr and Scott, I can see that they're enjoying it, too. They're doing a lot of pouring now. Flour, sugar and cocoa powder, I guess, judging by the packets strewn around.

Starr's got a white smudge across her nose and Scott puts his hands on her shoulders and turns her to face him. Then they both laugh and he delicately wipes it off with the end of a towel.

I turn back to my job, feeling a little like the *jealousy junkie* I once was*. But I got the wrong idea once before and I'm not going to spoil things now. They're

---

*Read *Jealousy Junkie* by Carrie Bright to find out how Maddy's jealousy made her fall out with Scott!

friends, and that's what friends do.

I mix in the sugar and dried fruit with my hands, followed by my grated apples.

'Now the eggs.' Nat passes them to me. 'Get cracking.'

'Er, what with? I haven't done this before. Don't you have some kind of egg-cracker thingy?'

'Nope – here's a chef's tip. If you bang two eggs together like this' – he picks up two eggs and taps them against one another – 'only one egg will break. Look!'

He shows me the eggs. One has a perfect crack in it which he somehow opens with his thumb, and releases the egg perfectly whole into the bowl.

'It doesn't matter if you crack the yolk, anyway. Here – have a go.'

I bang the eggs, one shatters and I spend the next five minutes fishing bits of eggshell out of the mixture.

'Shall we try a new recipe – crunchy apple cake?' I ask, holding the next eggs ready.

'Hmm – try cracking them on the side of this first.' Nat hands me a white, china bowl. 'Practice makes perfect.'

'Do I have to stir this round by hand, too?' I peer at the slimy, eggy mess, wondering if I can wear rubber gloves.

'Nope – use a wooden spoon, and make sure there are no dry areas of flour.'

'Yes, chef! And what are you doing there – what's that?'

'This is greaseproof paper – and this,' he holds up a flat, round piece of metal, 'is the base of a nine-inch spring-form tin.'

'A what tin?'

(Mad's note: All this cookery chat – Nat's either speaking in French or talking technical. It's very impressive!)

Nat puts the cake tin together. 'It goes in like that to bake,' he says. 'When it cools down, I release the spring and ease out the cake on its base. Oh – it helps to grease the sides of the tin first so it doesn't stick.'

'And I run a palette knife round the edge too,' Scott adds, from across the kitchen.

I look at him in amazement.

'Something my mum showed me!' he laughs.

'Top marks.' Nat give him the thumbs up.

My head is spinning with all this information. Luckily, once the eggs are mixed in we're done. Nat pours the mix into his tin and then the two cakes go in the oven.

'They'll take about an hour and a quarter.' Nat checks his watch. 'We've got cookery this afternoon, so I can get them out on time. Can you come back here after school to do the toppings? Then we can have a taster session.'

'Mmm, can't wait!' Starr says.

'Try to stop me!' Scott licks his lips. 'And they'll taste all the sweeter because we made them.'

I smile sadly, knowing I won't be there to share.

Tasty topping tips: chocolate cake treat

Use chocolate spread straight from the jar. Smother the cake top with it and then decorate with grated chocolate shavings.

11
RECIPE FOR SUCCESS

KEEP YOUR OWN RECIPE BOOK
Why not create your own recipe book, so you can keep all your favourite recipes in one place?

After school I get to the park early and sit on a bench near the bandstand, watching the world go by.

Nat will be with Scott and Starr now, giving them some excuse to explain why I can't be there for the cake tasting. I hate lying to them, but it sounds so lame to say my sweet tooth is out of control.

He said he'd meet me here for our walking session. I'm his fitty buddy and he's my foody friend.

(Mad's note: we also need a sense of humour workout.)

My brain is drained after that full-on cookery session, so I sit back and watch the scene. There are teenagers skateboarding, mums and dads taking their kids and dogs for a walk, the graffiti-covered shack and the bandstand with paint peeling off it...

Next thing I hear is a voice.

'Maddy? You OK?'

'W-what? W-who?' My eyes snap open. 'Oh, Nat... Sorry, just a bit tired, that's all. I'm fine now.' I stand up and start jumping up and down on the spot. 'Look – all ready for action! Had the power nap, now for the power walk.'

I head off towards the shack doing a silly walk, wiggling my bum like the marathon walkers do on TV, and Nat joins in. After a few circuits round the shack we collapse back onto the bench in a heap, laughing and wheezing.

'*Woooh!* I needed that,' I say, fanning my face, which is now glowing like a hotplate.

'Yeah, must have been tough today. Can't have been easy walking into the kitchen, not knowing how they'd take it. Everything worked out well, though, didn't it? And the cakes were *dee*-licious, even if I do say so myself.'

'So what did you say to Scott and Starr? Were they OK about me not going?'

'Oh, I just said you had to pick up your little brother from nursery. They were fine about it.'

'Are you sure? I still don't think they're quite the same with me – it's not like before.' A picture of Scott delicately brushing flour from Starr's face flashes into my mind as I speak.

Nat shakes his head. 'I didn't notice anything.'

'*Hmm*, but it does seem a bit odd – one minute I'm dead against the Great Cake Bake, and now I'm offering to help. I wouldn't blame them if they were still a bit unsure of me.'

'Nothing you can do about it, is there?' Nat leans back and puts his hands behind his head. 'Just relax.'

I try to but my mind whirrs like a mixer, stirring and rehashing thoughts and images. Then, faster than you can say *Double-Frosted Fudge Cake*, an idea takes shape.

I can see a wonderful celebration event, which will help the Fair Food cause, and – I hope – convince my friends to trust me again.

MADDY'S RECIPE FOR SUCCESS: PICNIC IN THE PARK

Ingredients

1 rundown park shack
1 stick of ginger Maddy – bursting with ideas
1 spoonful of Nat – for that fuller flavour
1 cup of Scott – keen as mustard
1 Starr – very artistic and decorative
Fair Food cakes (all varieties)
A pinch of adult advice

Method

Brush the park shack with fresh paint and leave to dry. Decorate with 'Café Open' sign.

Meanwhile, stir up the rest of the ingredients and simmer gently for a few weeks.

Pour into café, add publicity and serve on a Saturday.

Garnish with sunshine and music to taste.

'Nat, stand up for a minute.' I get to my feet and Nat joins me.

'Right, close your eyes. No peeking.'

'I can't help it!' He squints through one eye. 'What's going on?'

'Nothing to worry about – trust me.' I take off my scarf and tie it across his eyes like a blindfold.

'What the...?'

'*Shhh*, you have to keep quiet. Now, tell me. What can you hear?'

He listens for a moment. 'Kids shouting, skateboards, wind in the trees, dogs barking...'

'Good. Now think about it. Those children are using up energy, and so are their mums and dads. They're getting very hungry and thirsty. *Mmm*, what they need is a nice cup of coffee and a piece of home-made cake... Or soup and a sandwich. Even the dogs might want a snack or a bowl of water – but where are they going to get it?'

'Dunno,' Nat shrugs. 'On the High Street in town?'

'No. They don't have to go all that way because there's a café in the park. It sells good food using local and Fair Food ingredients. And on a sunny day they can sit outside and listen to music, too. Maybe Starr's dad strumming the guitar – who knows?'

I untie the scarf from round his eyes and he blinks in the fading spring light. Then he sees what I see and a huge grin spreads across his face.

'It's there!' he points to the shack. 'And there are all the customers!' he points to a kid on a skateboard who sticks his tongue out. 'Maddy, that's genius! You've got your Big Idea!'

Next thing I know we're jumping up and down on the spot.

'It might be a bit extreme to imagine that Starr's dad would run the café...' I say breathlessly.

'No! Big Ideas have to be extreme – he's looking for a place, so why not here?'

'Needs a lot of work.' I stop jumping and come back down to planet Earth. 'Especially if it's going to be ready for the Great Cake Bake Week.'

'Well, we've got twenty-one days till then, and what a way to finish. We could open up the café on the Saturday so everyone can invite their families. Scott will love it – a real community event.'

At the mention of Scott I panic. 'Yes, but who does the shack belong to? How do you find out? Where do you start with stuff like this? What if Scott thinks it's a half-baked idea?'

I slump on the bench in a heap like someone knocked all the stuffing out of me. 'Shall we just forget it? It sounds too much like hard work!'

'You're right, it does.' Nat sits next to me. 'But that doesn't mean we shouldn't try.'

'Yeah, I suppose...'

'We've got all the ingredients in place here. And if it doesn't work out, Scott and Starr can see you've had a go. Come on, Maddy – you can't make an omelette without breaking eggs...'

And I can't help laughing. It all comes back to food with Nat. 'Yes, chef!'

'Good!' He gives me a hug and I hug him back.

Then we both realise what we're doing and – quicker than you can say *Easy Apple Cake* – we break free again.

12

JUST DESSERTS

> **USE FAIR FOOD PRODUCTS WHEREVER POSSIBLE IN YOUR RECIPES.**
> *You'll help growers get just what they deserve for their hard work.*

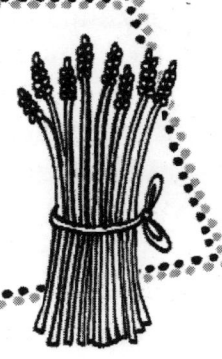

I resolve to tell Scott my Big Idea when he calls for me to walk to school. If he doesn't turn up, that means things still aren't right between us and I won't risk it.

So it's a big relief when the doorbell rings at eight o'clock and Max rushes up to my room, calling over and over, 'Maddy! Maddy! For you! For you!'

I bound down the stairs two at a time, open the front door wide and – surprise! Both Scott and Starr are standing together.

'Hi,' I say, trying to sound casual, but noting that they have moved away from each other slightly. 'What brings you both here?'

'Hey, thought we'd surprise you!' Scott sounds friendly enough and gives me a wide smile.

'I moved in with my grandparents last night,' Starr shrugs. 'Much as I love them, it's a bit of a squash, but at least it's nearer school and your place is on my way.'

'Yeah – it's just round the corner, as I found out yesterday. How many clothes do you need, Starr? I'm sure my arms are longer after shifting all those boxes.'

Starr laughs. 'It wasn't all clothes – there were books in there, too. You were a big help, Scott – sorry if they were a bit heavy.'

Scott flexes his muscles. 'You see how it is, Maddy. I'm only wanted for my muscle, not my mind.'

As they start joking around I can't help feeling just a touch left out. *Why didn't Starr ask me to help, too?* Then I remember that I didn't show up for the cake topping and tasting session last night. Yes, that would explain it.

(Mad's note: Phew – close call. Just avoided an embarrassing Jealousy Junkie outburst...)

We set off walking and I decide to come right out with my new *Recipe for Success* – as Nat called it – before it goes stale.

'Guess what? I've got an idea for how to finish off the Great Cake Bake Week in style. How d'you fancy selling cakes at a café in the park?'

I wait for the groans but they don't happen. Instead, two eager faces are fixed on me, their eyes hungry for more.

By the time we reach the school gates I've given them

everything, even down to my vision of Starr's dad playing music outside in the summer. They both know the park and think it's a great idea.

'You go in.' Starr waves us through the gates. 'I'm going to call him right now. Dad's looking for a place to manage and I think he could go for it!'

Scott and I wander into school and it feels like old times.

'Have you noticed how she doesn't call him Matt any more since the split?' I say. 'He's "Dad" now, isn't he? That's so cool.'

Scott stops at his locker. 'She loves him and so she worries about him, too.' He gets out his books and then turns to me. 'This café is your best idea yet. If he takes it on it could be a lifeline for him. For both of them.'

He's got his intense and caring *I'm-a-future-lawyer* face on now, and it's making me anxious.

'Oh, erm, many a slip between cup and lip and...er...don't count your chickens before they're hatched!' I mumble, getting nervous and resorting to food and drink comparisons.

'What—?'

Before Scott can quiz me Starr comes running up, breathless and glowing.

'It's a yes – he wants to see it! He's going to meet us in the park tonight to see the café.'

'Shack,' I correct her, worried they might not see it as I do. 'It's not a café yet. You'll see...'

'Is that it?' Scott stares at the graffiti-covered walls and boarded windows, looking very unimpressed. Starr says nothing but I can see she's disappointed too.

'You've got to use your imagination!' Nat says, walking closer. 'Ignore the rain and think of it on a sunny day, tables outside and—'

'Sorry I'm late, guys.'

Starr's dad appears, looking very smart in a dark velvet jacket and black jeans – a change from his usual faded denim and ripped t-shirts. He still looks like a rock star, with his zipped-up guitar slung over his back. He dangles a set of keys and walks over to the padlocked door on the shack.

'I had to speak with a lot of Town Hall pen-pushers,' he explains. 'At first they were having none of it – said this place was due to be pulled down.'

He pauses to put the key in the padlock. 'But then I told them about your Fair Food idea and it suddenly ticked all their boxes. Yes!'

He takes off the chain and unlocks the door. 'Come on in. They told me the electric was off, so I brought a torch.'

We all pile inside and a single beam picks out the empty, unloved interior. There's an overturned chair, an abandoned box and little else.

'I used to come here as a kid, you know.' The beam

of light darts around like a firefly, picking out points of interest. 'I remember when I had to stand on tip-toes to peer over that counter – my Nan used to bring me here for a drink and a biscuit.'

The beam moves over to a door at the back. 'There's room for a fridge and a cooker in there. This café was always a bit old-fashioned, but people loved it! Old men playing dominoes outside... I'd love to do a summer gig in there with a few of my mates.'

My eyes have adjusted a little to the dark and I see Starr walk over to her father. 'It's such a lot of work, Dad – why make life difficult for yourself? It was only an idea to finish off our Great Cake Bake Week – we don't *have* to do it.'

'Are you kidding, Starr?' The beam of light flickers up and down and left to right like a laser show. 'It's perfect. When you and Scott told me about this Fair Food project last night...well, call me an old hippy, but it sounded like you wanted to change the world. Now this place comes up, so count me in.'

Starr gives him a hug. 'You *are* an old hippy, Dad. Oh no – you're not going to sing about it, are you?'

'What makes you think I'd do a thing like that?' he says, slinging his guitar around and unzipping the cover.

He hands her the torch. 'Now here's one I made up in the Town Hall, waiting for those pen-pushers to see sense. It's called "Just Desserts"...'

'JUST DESSERTS'

There's a place you can go from dawn to dark –

Come and visit our café in the park!

We got home-baked cakes and the tastiest food

To fill you up and make you feel good.

Help those farmers home and away

To get fair treatment and fair pay.

They don't always get it and that's what hurts –

Eat here and they'll get their just desserts.

Starr shines the torch on her dad like a spotlight and we all clap when he finishes.

Suddenly everything seems possible, and transforming this rundown shack into a café sounds like a piece of cake.

(Mad's note: Hmmm – I only hope it works as well as Nat's recipes.)

13

PASSION CAKE

Nat's Passion Cake

This is a great cake to celebrate with!

You'll need:

2 small Fair Food bananas (mashed)

2 large locally grown carrots (grated)

200 g Fair Food brown sugar

200 ml sunflower oil

250 g self-raising flour

3 eggs (local hens)

50 g chopped Fair Food walnuts

50 g dried Fair Food coconut

50 g Fair Food raisins

1 tsp ground cinnamon

'Any news?' I ask Starr a week later.

We're in the school kitchen where all the Cake Bake volunteers meet for a big bake-fest two or three times a week.

I'm grating carrots and mashing bananas for a passion cake, which sounds heavenly. Luckily the finished cakes go in the freezer – so I'm not tempted to raid the kitchen for the odd slice in between classes.

'Business plan,' Starr says. 'That's the first thing. Then he has to go to the bank and talk to them nicely about a loan. Then the council want him to fill in loads of forms and... Oh, I don't know. The way it's going, I don't think Dad's got a chance of opening the café on time.'

'Two weeks to the Great Cake Bake Sale and counting,' Scott says.

'Yes, but the café doesn't have to be open till the end of the week,' I remind him.

He nods. 'That gives him at least five days extra. So, yeah, you're right, that's loads of time.'

Even as he says it Starr sighs and Scott goes over to give her a hug.

'Better get on,' she says, looking at me awkwardly, and I wonder why. Is she regretting this café idea after all?

I suddenly feel the urge to plunge a wooden spoon into a bowl of creamy topping lurking on the next table.

Creamy topping and filling

You'll need:

* 100 g butter
* 100 g light soft cream cheese
* 250 g icing sugar
* 2 tsp lemon juice

Beat all the ingredients together until the mixture is light and fluffy.

DESSERT DIVA

'You still up for a power walk after this?' Nat appears by my side just as the tasty topping is about to reach my lips.

'Oh, Nat. I, er, didn't see you there!' I say, as the spoon clatters onto the counter. 'Yes, see you at the school gates and...er, thanks.'

I mop up the spilt creamy topping and return – gratefully – to carrot-grating.

Two weeks whirr by in a blur of cake-baking, power-walking and swimming. Nat's very good at keeping up his exercise plan and he helps me keep up my no-cake ban.

The only fly in the soup is the café idea. I've stopped asking about it now – there's hardly any time left, and from what Starr told me, her Dad is still tied up with complicated paperwork.

'These are the final cakes, people,' Nat announces on the Friday before the Great Cake-Bake Sale starts. He opens the oven and pulls out a tray of freshly baked cakes and the warm, sweet, spicy smell fills the kitchen.

(Mad's note: Mmm, if someone could bottle that smell, the perfume would be worth millions!)

I have to get some fresh air before I pass out. It's been so long since I ate a cake that I'm drooling already. Just as I reach the door, Starr calls out,

'Maddy, can you meet us at the café tomorrow morning? Dad's got some good news!' Her cheeks are glowing from the heat of the kitchen and she looks happier than I've seen her for ages.

Make it from the heart and this passion cake never fails!

* Heat the oven to 180°C (350°F, Gas Mark 4).

* Mix together the flour, sugar, oil, eggs and cinnamon in a bowl.

* Fold in the carrots, bananas, coconut, nuts and raisins.

* Pour the mixture into two 20 cm tins and bake for 35 minutes.

* Cool on wire racks before adding the filling and topping.

I nod and wave, then run down the corridor like I'm being chased by demons – sweet and sugary dessert demons, the type that get into your blood and won't let you go.

Next morning, Nat and I power-walk through the park to the café. We can hear guitar music strumming as we head towards it and the door is open.

'Surprise!' Starr calls as we enter. Already it looks brighter because the boards have been taken down from the windows, although some have been smashed and need replacing.

'Meet the new owner!' Scott says.

Starr's dad stops playing his music and comes over to shake our hands. 'Well, technically the bank is the new owner until I pay off the loan,' he smiles. 'But I've got a year to prove we can make it work.'

'So, when d'you plan to open?' I look around – the floors have been swept but it's still got a very long way to go before that can happen.

He shrugs. 'Sorry guys, I really wanted to be open for the end of your Great Cake Bake, but—'

'Yeah, and this weekend we break up for Easter. So if you do open we can help out in the holidays. That would really get this place off to a good start.' Scott's got his business head on and there's no stopping him now.

'I don't know, it's a lot of work. It'll take at least three weeks, I reckon.'

'We can all help out,' Nat offers. 'It just needs a lick of paint.'

'Yeah — piece of cake,' I say.

'A walk in the park...' Scott winks at me.

'This is what I told them at the bank!' Starr's dad starts strumming again. 'I said, these young people have got passion.' His strumming turns into the "Just Desserts" song.

'Dad, no!' Starr buries her head in her hands with embarrassment as her dad starts humming.

'Do we have a name for this café?' I whisper, thinking about the publicity angle.

'*Just Desserts* – that's what I'd like to call this place.' Starr's Dad stops playing. 'It says what we're about – giving farmers what they deserve – and we've already got the theme song to go with it.'

'But there's already a factory in Westfield called Just Desserts. Maddy worked there, didn't you?' Scott jumps in and looks at me for backup.

'Are you kidding? No one could ever confuse that huge, faceless Fake-Bake factory with a small, friendly Fair Food café.'

'Well, Dad is the owner, so...' Starr looks as if she's willing me to agree.

'*Just Desserts* – why not?' I say, waiting for Scott to say something.

He doesn't. He looks lost in thought, and a frown-line appears between his brows.

DESSERT DIVA

I don't know why – but calling this café *Just Desserts* has suddenly given me my best idea yet...

(Mad's note: But will this idea be the icing on the cake, or the mould in the middle?)

14

FEED YOUR SOUL

Come to the grand opening of Just Desserts Café

The café in the park that will feed your soul – as well as your stomach!
All cakes are made from Fair Food products,
e.g. coffee, chocolate, sugar, bananas and nuts,
to give farmers in other countries a fair share
of the profits.
(Their just deserts!)
We also use local ingredients
like eggs, carrots and milk to keep farms near us
in business.
Profits from food sold on Saturday
and Sunday will go to Fair Food.

Scott contacts other School Council members, who help us sweep up and paint walls at the weekend. Meanwhile, a few friends of Starr's dad turn up and do the serious stuff, like replacing windows and sorting out the electrical fittings in the kitchen.

By Sunday night we've made good progress but we're nowhere near finished. Nat's fixed us all a hot drink (we now have a kettle and a fridge) and we sit around on dustsheets for a final planning meeting.

'OK, next week we have to focus on selling cakes at school,' Scott says. 'We're doing this project to raise funds for Fair Food, so we need to be behind the cake stalls at break-time and lunchtime. I've drawn up a rota – here it is.'

He passes it around and I notice my name isn't on there – neither is Nat's.

'Nat, most of us will be busy selling cakes next week, but one or two people will help you make them. So you'll be supervising the cake-baking team in the kitchen at lunchtime and after school. We're going to need a lot more cakes!'

'Yes, boss.'

'Maddy, you'll lead on publicity. Write some snappy text with a great slogan and take it to the Resource Centre for printing. Start giving out leaflets by Tuesday or Wednesday at the latest – I'll find someone to help you.'

'Yep – I've had an idea already. We could make invitations and send them out to—'

'Do what you think's best,' Scott interrupts. 'We want families flocking to this café at the weekend. You've done publicity before, and it worked, so you're in charge.'

I nod, pleased at Scott's faith in me, but slightly nervous, too, because I don't want to let him down.

'What about the café?' Nat asks. 'We've done a lot this weekend, but it's still not exactly ready to go.'

'My mates are going to help out – don't you worry.' Starr's dad strums his guitar dramatically. 'They're so impressed with you lot and your ideas that they want to help. They're coming along after work next week to kit it out.'

He starts playing his guitar, looking relaxed and happy.

'Some of those mates were in a band with Dad years ago,' Starr stage-whispers over the music. 'They're talking of reforming and making a comeback!'

She shakes her head and smiles – as if she's the parent, and her dad's the teenager with mad ideas.

When I get home later that night I start work straightaway...

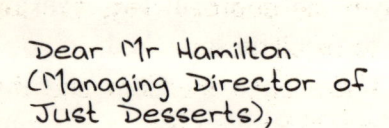

Dear Mr Hamilton
(Managing Director of
Just Desserts),

We hope you can come along to our café opening on Saturday. It is called Just Desserts, but it's not to be confused with your factory!
The name relates to the Fair Food products we use so farmers are paid what they deserve for their work.
We'll be happy to tell you more about it on the day - an invitation is enclosed.

Hope you can make it!

Your sincerely,

Maddy Blue

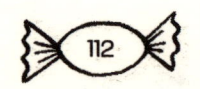

By the Friday of the Great Cake Bake week we're all very happy. The cakes are selling at school, posters and leaflets are everywhere and the café is almost ready.

So that morning, when the doorbell rings as usual, I expect Scott and Starr to be all smiles.

I gallop downstairs, throw open the door and then stop – my stomach flipping like a pancake.

Starr's in tears and Scott's standing with his arm round her.

'What is it? What's wrong? D'you want to come in?'

'No, it's OK, I'm fine,' sobs Starr, who clearly isn't. 'We've got to get to school to sort out the cakes.'

I run back into the house to get some tissues (well, kitchen roll – it's all we've got), and Starr blows her nose and scrubs her face.

Scott still has his arm around her. 'You OK? Ready to move on?' he murmurs, tilting her chin so she looks into his eyes.

I'm starting to feel like a spare part all of a sudden, but she nods and he drops his arm so we can all start walking.

'My dad had a letter from the Just Desserts factory,' Starr begins. 'They don't want him to open tomorrow.'

'They said he was in breach of trademark law by using the name Just Desserts,' Scott explains, sounding like a lawyer already.

'Oh.' I blush guiltily, wondering if this has anything to do with the invitation I sent out. Then I get an idea.

'So if he changes the name he can still open?'

'In theory, yes,' Scott agrees. 'But he's not going to do that, is he?'

Starr sighs. 'He got the letter this morning and ripped it up – says he's not going to be bullied by a faceless company with no values!'

'Good for him!' I can't help admiring Starr's dad for not backing down.

Even Starr smiles for a second. 'Yes, I know it's great that he's taking a stand, but it could land him in deep trouble.'

'So what can they do to him?' It's break-time now and I've braved the kitchen to tell Nat all about what happened.

The air is warm and sweet. It smells of vanilla, chocolate, orange and sugar, all mingled together to make my taste buds tingle.

I'm cake-deprived and feeling stressed – a blend of ingredients that makes me crave about seventeen desserts right now. And still have room for pudding.

'Scott says they could take him to court,' I continue. 'If he loses he'll have a huge fine to pay out – and he owes money already.'

'But why would a big company like Just Desserts even bother about a little café in the local park? It doesn't make sense.'

'Maybe it's because I sent their Managing Director

an invitation!' I confess, the words tumbling out. 'I thought he'd be flattered we took the same name. I even thought they might learn something about Fair Food if they came to the café.'

I hang my head, fighting back tears of frustration – what with the worry about Starr's dad and trying not to eat anything in here.

Of course, Nat's lovely. He comes over and hugs me. He smells of apple, sugar and cinnamon – I could stay here forever.

'Scott and Starr trusted me with the publicity and now I feel like I've let them down,' I mutter into his apron.

'No, you haven't. You were doing your job. And getting a big factory like that involved – it's genius!'

'What?' I lift my head up to see if he's joking.

'Listen – if our cake sales can help Fair Food, just think what would happen if a big factory agreed to buy their products. That would make a massive difference!'

'But it's not going to happen, is it?' I move away from Nat. 'That's what I was hoping for, too, but instead of getting the factory on our side they're taking us to court! Well, Starr's dad, anyway. It's a mess.'

'Come on, Maddy, don't give up now. You're the one with all the ideas – how can we persuade this man to change his mind?'

Nat looks at me with his melted chocolate eyes and I say the first thing that drops into my mind.

'Chocolate kisses.'

'Sorry?' Nat looks confused.

'*Umm*, well, that's just my name for them. You know those chocolate truffles you left in my bag...' My face grows hot. 'Well, I *think* it was you?'

Nat looks as hot and bothered as me now. 'Handmade chocolate truffles...yeah, that was me,' he mutters.

'Oooh, they were so *lush*,' I say, reliving the memory. 'They lingered on my lips and melted in my mouth.'

Nat's dark eyes widen and I stop.

'Anyway, that's why I called them chocolate kisses...' I smile lamely. 'And my mum always says that the way to a man's heart is through his stomach, so—'

'Didn't work with you, though,' Nat mumbles, turning away and starting to chop up some butter.

'Nat, I...'

'Don't worry – maybe it's because you're not a man. Ha! So what's the plan? We make some for him and take them round?'

'Exactly – as an apology. Go after school and ask him to think again. Give him a peace offering. Hopefully he'll taste the difference between your chocolate kisses and those chemically enhanced cakes he makes.'

'OK – I accept your chocolate challenge!' Nat opens a drawer and pulls out a bar of Fair Food chocolate. 'I'll have to melt this with some cream and butter now – it needs to rest in the fridge for a couple of hours before we make the truffles.'

'Really?' I squeak, my mouth drooling at the thought of it.

'Yeah, so meet me in the kitchen after school. We're going to make some *soul* food.'

I nod. 'OK, then. But don't let even one chocolate kiss pass my lips – promise?'

'I promise,' he says, sadly.

15

CHOCOLATE KISSES

These truffles make the perfect present. Put them in a box tied with a ribbon to create an extra special gift!

Ingredients
250 g Fair Food dark chocolate (min 70% cocoa solids)
125 ml double cream (from local farms)
25 g butter (from local farms)
1 tbsp vanilla essence (optional)
50 g cocoa powder to roll truffles in

DESSERT DIVA

It's only ten in the morning but the park is filling up with families. The weather's on our side, too. The spring sunshine is so warm that we've put tables outside with bunches of daffodils and tulips on them – donated by the park keeper.

So we have all the ingredients for a perfect day... Except for the fact that at any minute now we could be threatened with legal action and told to close.

Unfortunately we didn't get to see the Managing Director last night after all. When we turned up at the Just Desserts factory with our chocolate kisses he was in a meeting, so we left them at reception with a note.

(Mad's note: So will today be a recipe for success or disaster? The proof of the pudding is in the eating...)

Scott, Starr, her dad, Nat and I have been here for two hours already. We've decorated the tables, put our cakes on the counter in glass domes, and got the water urns filled and bubbling.

'Are we *mise en place*, chef?' I ask Nat, showing off my new French phrase.

'All set.'

'OK, guys – good luck. This is it!' Starr's dad unlocks the door and our first customers pile in.

It makes me feel so proud to serve the cakes we've all had a go at making. And everyone is so enthusiastic about them. When the customers come through the doors and see all the different cakes there are lots of *Ooohs!* and *Aaahs!* – and that's from the adults, not the children.

'Chocolate cake, apple cake, passion cake, coffee and

walnut – what would you like?' The words drip from my lips like honey.

The first few lucky customers even get a chocolate kiss with their coffee – we had some left over from last night's emergency batch.

How to make chocolate kisses

* Break the chocolate into tiny pieces and place them in a bowl.
* Heat the cream in a saucepan until it reaches boiling point.
* Add the butter and take the pan off the heat.
* Microwave the chocolate for a few seconds until soft.
* Pour the cream and butter over the chocolate and stir gently together.
* Leave to stand for a few minutes and stir again.
* Cover and place in the fridge for two or three hours.
* Scoop out little balls of the set truffle mixture.
* Shape the truffles in the palm of your hand and then roll them in cocoa powder.
* You could also use icing sugar, chopped nuts or even chocolate shavings to coat the truffles. Mmm!

When my mum and dad turn up with Max his eyes are like marbles as he peers on tiptoe at the cake counter.

'My sister made all these cakes,' he tells anyone who'll listen.

(Mad's note: And who am I to shatter a young boy's illusions?)

All this running around is a great workout and there's no time to comfort eat.

As I clear up plates people keep stopping me to say how lovely the cakes are and can they have the recipe? That's my next idea – a Just Desserts cookbook!

By two o'clock I'm starting to relax. No police, no lawyers. No one. Perhaps the threatening words were nothing but hot air?

'Come on, sit down and take a break with me,' Nat offers. 'It's your turn – most people have had one already.'

The tables outside are still full. Starr's dad is strumming his guitar at the top of the bandstand steps and waves us over, so we go and perch on the bottom step.

Nat offers me a piece of cake. 'Try this – it's the best ever, even if I do say so myself. Passion cake.'

'No thanks, I've just had some soup.' I wave it away

as my stomach gurgles with desire. It looks fresh and creamy and utterly, utterly lush.

'Sorry, yeah, I understand. No sweet treats. I do admire your willpower, Maddy...I just thought, you know, as it's a celebration...'

I look away, feeling mean-spirited. If only he knew that I've got no willpower at all. One sweet slip and I'll be on a sugar splurge for the rest of the day – I know it.

He's the sweetest boy I've ever met but all I do is reject him – or at least his food – and it makes me feel worse each time.

'Nat, I—'

Just then Starr's dad strums some familiar chords.

'They're playing our "Just Desserts" song,' Nat smiles.

'Yeah.'

'I want to say a big thank you to these four people here,' Starr's dad speaks into a microphone that has appeared from nowhere. 'They're showing us the future of food – where to get it, how to make it, and best of all, how to enjoy eating it.'

Everyone claps as Scott, Starr, Nat and I give a wave and then clap each other, too.

'This Fair Food café is also going to be the future for me and my daughter, and for that I'm very grateful. Thank you all for coming and we hope to see you back at Just Desserts time after time. Here's the reason why – *one, two, three...*'

> *There's a place you can go*
> *from dawn to dark –*
> *Come and visit our café in the park!*
> *We got home-baked cakes and the tastiest food*
> > *To fill you up and make you feel good.*
>
> > *Help those farmers home and away*
> > *To get fair treatment and fair pay.*
> *They don't always get it and that's what hurts –*
> *Eat here and they'll get their just desserts.*

Starr, Scott, Nat and I all join in – whether it's cheesy or not – and as the last chords of the guitar fade away, it looks like everything is going to be all right...

'One question!' A man in dark glasses and a suit suddenly stands up. He's sitting at a table with two other men dressed the same way.

'Can you explain why you are using the registered trademark *Just Desserts* in your song?' the man continues. 'And, even more importantly, as the name of your café?'

He points to the doorway, where *Just Desserts* is painted in a rainbow of letters.

A hush falls over everyone. All I can hear is the soft swishing of the breeze in the trees.

Starr's dad speaks slowly into the mic. 'And why are you so interested?'

The man bows his head. 'I'm Travis Hamilton Junior. My father is the MD – Managing Director – of a large cake company near here, Just Desserts.'

'You're welcome to my café and our Great Cake Bake fundraiser,' Starr's dad says politely.

'Thank you. I asked my father if I could check it out. Quite frankly I'm surprised you have opened the café. I take it you received the letter warning of legal action if you did so?'

'We did, yes, but I refuse to give in to the bully-boy tactics of a faceless corporation.'

There's a sharp intake of breath all round at this. Mr Hamilton doesn't look as angry as I'd expected; he just looks saddened.

'I have no quarrel with you and what you are doing – in fact, I admire it. But not only did you steal our name for your café, you invited us to the opening. How do you explain that?'

Starr's dad hesitates and looks at his daughter. She looks at Scott and he looks at me – cringing on the bottom step trying to hide behind Nat.

He gives me a nudge. 'Go on, Maddy – now's your chance. Just be yourself and tell them like you told me.'

I stand up, shaking like a jelly, and someone passes me the mic.

'Mr Hamilton, thank you for coming to Just Desserts café today. I worked and ate at your factory and I love your food – in fact, I can't get enough of it. But I invited you to Just Desserts so you could see there are other ways to make cakes. We're not a factory – my friends baked the cakes themselves. They didn't use any chemicals or preservatives, just local and Fair Food ingredients. That way you don't just get good food, but the profits go back to the farmers who grow it. And who can argue with that?'

I pause while he digests my words.

'So I thought you'd be pleased we took your name, and' – my voice fades to a whisper – 'and hoped you'd think it's such a great idea that you'd want to help.'

Everyone claps as I sit down, covered in confusion. What's going to happen now? I've just admitted to stealing his company name and he's got the law on his side.

Will it be handcuffs?

A straightjacket?

(Mad's note: Or – considering my mouth – more likely a gagging order.)

Mr Hamilton stands up. 'Thank you, Maddy Blue. I believe it was you who sent us those chocolate truffles? Delicious, by the way.'

I nod.

'Well, now, Just Desserts prides itself on listening to its

customers, and there might be something in what you say. But one thing troubles me...'

He pauses dramatically and I wait for his next words. He's been far too nice – there has to be a catch somewhere...

Mr Hamilton raises his arm and points at me. 'You have already said how much you like our factory cakes – yes?'

I nod again.

'But I saw that young man there offer you a slice of home-baked cake and you refused. Not one single bite. Why not?'

All eyes are on me now – and there's nowhere to hide.

16

EAT CAKE AND CELEBRATE!

Eating yourself fit should not be a life-sentence of misery.

We say eat cake! Celebrate when you feel the need!

Yes, why not? I must admit it doesn't look good. As a Dessert Diva I should have been first in the queue.

Why can't I have just one cake? It's good food made with the best ingredients and by Nat's own fair hands.

(Mad's note: But one good cake leads to another in Mad-World, and will I know when to stop?)

I can't tell everyone about my crazy cravings — it sounds so lame — but I have to say something. '*Um,*

I haven't had any cake because…er, well, it's for the customers,' I shrug.

'Very noble,' Mr Hamilton nods. 'Tell you what – there's a piece of cake there. Why don't you eat it now and tell me what you truly think? Is it better than the cakes you love from the Just Desserts factory?'

Well, I can hardly start screaming for the cake police, can I?

> *Help! Get that sweet treat away from me or I'll go crazy! Out of control! No dessert, cake or pudding will be safe after this!*

'OK, it's a deal,' I say, sounding more confident than I feel. 'Nat, please could you pass me that large piece of passion cake over there?'

He hands me the slice he offered earlier and whispers, 'Enjoy!'

I stare at the cake on my plate.

The last few months I've been stressing and obsessing about what to eat and what not to eat.

It's given me food for thought…

Food is fuel to Flat-Pack Zac.
Food is politics to Scott.
Food is love to Mum.
Food is a living to Starr's dad and all the farmers who grow it.

Watching everyone eating and sharing food together today has made me think. *Why am I a cake-hater? What's happened to me? That's not who I am – I'm a Dessert Diva...*

Enjoy, Nat said. And that's what I'll do. *Eat cake and celebrate!*

'What's wrong, Maddy Blue? Aren't you going to eat it?' Mr Hamilton's voice jolts me out of my daydream.

I lift my fork up high in the air, plunge it into the cake and shovel a massive mouthful into my mouth.

'MMMMMM. *Mmmmmm, mmmmmm.*' I polish it off in moments, picking up the last crumbs with my fingers. 'That is the most delicious, heavenly, lip-smackingly moreish cake I have ever tasted. In fact – is there any *more?*' I hold out my plate for second helpings...

Everyone cheers as Mr Hamilton walks over. He shakes hands with Nat, Scott, Starr and her dad in turn.

Then he comes over to me and speaks into my mic.

'No one – not even the greatest actor in the world – could fake that passion cake passion! I've been looking for a project to call my own for some time now, and I'd like to take this back to Dad. I can't promise anything yet, but we'll talk!'

He shakes my hand and noise erupts all around me. Not that I take any notice. I've got a date with more cake and I want it *now!*

'Um, are you sure you want another piece, Maddy?'

Nat and I are in the kitchen and he's looking for more passion cake. I think I've just had the last two slices.

'Yes! No! Oh, I don't know! What's wrong with me? Why can't I be like normal people and stop at one treat?'

'Maddy, I—'

Suddenly the door bursts open. 'Here you are! We've been looking for you everywhere!'

With one look at Scott and Starr I remember the invitation I sent to the Just Desserts factory.

'OK, I know – really stupid move. What was I thinking, sending the invite to Mr Just Desserts? It was—'

'No – it was inspired. Thanks to you we've got a result!' Scott and Starr dance around the room like popcorn on a hotplate.

'Tell her, Starr,' Scott says when they're all danced-out and stand together arm in arm.

(*Mad's note: It could be cake-cravings clouding my mind, but these two are like cookies and cream – just meant for each other!*)

'Mr Hamilton called his dad and got the go-ahead for a six-month trial. He wants to know the most popular cakes and desserts we sell at the café. Then his factory will bring out a special line of Fair Food desserts. It's only small-scale to start off with, but it should make a difference.'

'They'll have special labels explaining where the ingredients come from and how we bake and test them out in our café.'

'So Starr's dad gets paid as well as the farmers. They also get guaranteed orders in future. It's a win-win situation. I always believed in you, Maddy!' Scott looks at me and I hit him.

Playfully.

Well, playfully hard – like a brother–sister kind of thing.

'No, you didn't!' I say. 'But, just this once, I forgive you!'

'Thank you, oh special one!' Scott bows down pretending to worship me. Then he gets up, saying, 'Oh, and I forgive you, too.'

'Thanks – and, er, since when did you and Starr become an item?'

Starr blushes and Scott squirms awkwardly.

'We didn't want to tell you in case you thought you'd be left out,' Starr says. 'But we'd never do that.'

'Never.' Scott finally looks at me.

I smile – we go back a long way and I believe him.

'Dad asked if we all wanted to help out some weekends at the café. He'll pay us! Are you up for that?' Starr's eyes are shining and she's got her old glow back.

'Yeah, and we need this *Food Dude* and his skills as well as our *Dessert Diva*. What d'you say?'

Scott and Starr look at us both. I can see they still want us all to be friends, but it won't be the same type of friendship now they're a couple.

I don't feel jealous any more, just a bit sad. Things change. And they're lucky to have found each other.

'Well, I can't cook that well, but I can wait tables,' I offer.

'OK, deal. Gotta go now – said we'd help my dad load up his car. We'll meet up later, OK?'

When they're gone Nat looks at me. 'How you feeling?'

'I don't know. Churned up like I've been put through a mixer. I'm happy this Fair Food project worked out so well and I've got my friends back too, but...'

'Still got those sweet tooth cravings? Shall I see if there are any cakes left outside?'

I giggle. 'You're the only person who knows about my secret cravings. I get so upset about them, but hearing you now it just sounds funny.'

I start running around the room, going, *'Help! My sweet tooth's out of control!'*

'Situation critical.' Nat talks into an imaginary walkie-talkie. *'We need desserts here, or cake or chocolate!'*

He turns to me. 'Sorry, nothing left.'

'Arggghhh!' I collapse onto the floor and slump against a cupboard.

'You OK?' Nat sits next to me and suddenly sounds serious.

'Oh, don't mind me. And thanks for listening. I just get so scared of my eating going out of control.

Remember the cake factory? All those cakes rumbling towards us? Well, I still have nightmares about it. It's stupid, I know—'

'It's not stupid at all, but I think that cutting out all these sweet treats is making you a bit of a yo-yo dieter.'

'Really? What's that? I don't even eat yo-yos.'

'Ha-ha. It's when you cut out eating something completely, so you end up wanting it more and more. Like you and sweet treats. That's why you get cravings. When you finally let go your poor body doesn't know what's happening.'

'You mean I'm not freaky – these cravings are normal because of my healthy-eating plan?'

DON'T FEAST AND FAST!

Ninety-one percent of females have food cravings, according to a recent study – so you're not alone.

Manage your cravings by giving yourself some treats as part of a healthy-eating and exercise plan.

'Healthy eating? You wouldn't go near anything sweet, would you – but I've been reading this magazine and you can have cakes and desserts now and again.'

'You're right. I just don't trust myself, that's all.

I don't know what to do about it.'

'I told you – let me be your foody friend! You're my fitty buddy and that's worked out really well. A foody friend doesn't just show you how to bake cakes – it's someone you can talk to when things get tough – to help you tame those cravings.'

'Yeah, I'd like that. You're the first person I've told about my scary secret cravings, and even talking about it like this is making me feel better.'

'I can even show you how to bake healthy sweet treats...if you want.'

'Yeah, and that soup, too. You said it was easy.'

'Deal. You've got to make friends with food, dude! Sure you don't want me to rustle up a cake right now?'

I shake my head. 'Not a cake, but what about those chocolate kisses? You got any of those left?'

And now I'm not just thinking of the handmade truffles in the heart-shaped box, but of the words written inside it. *Be my Valentine*. I hope he gets the hint.

'Nope, they take a bit longer to make. We could buy some chocolate and—'

'It's not so much the chocolate part I'm craving,' I whisper, feeling suddenly shy but sure of myself, too. 'It's the other bit...'

'Ah,' Nat looks at me nervously. '*Erm*, really? You mean the *kis*—'

I nod.

'Sweet! But I, *um*, don't know the recipe. I, er...haven't

had much practice.'

'Me neither, but we've got all the right ingredients, haven't we? One *Food Dude* and one *Dessert Diva* – I'm sure we can work it out...'

(Mad's note: A moment on the lips and nothing on the hips. Perfect!)

Maddy

Have you read the previous Maddy books?

Jealousy Junkie

Can Maddy's mags help when she fails an Envy Exam and falls out with her best friends?
Blusherama!

Gothic Goddess

Maddy's stars say she has a hot date with Fate – then a tall, dark, Goth-gorgeous guy walks into her life.
Omigoth!

Read on for an enticing JEALOUSY JUNKIE taster...

1
FRIENDSHIP FORECAST

Leo
Two's company but is three a crowd?
There's a shooting star zooming into your planetary area. It means a new person will enter your life, but can an old friendship stand the test?

Wear something sparkly for luck.

Spooooky!
Last night I painted my toe nails with sparkly nail polish for the first time ever! It's a sign – a sparkly sign!

OK so it was a free gift with this mag but so what? According to my stars someone new is going to zap into my life.

'Maddy – Scott's here!' Mum shouts up.

I close my mag, cram it in my school bag and go downstairs in my usual daze.

Who can this new person possibly be? And what did Destiny Dreamer mean, *'can an old friendship stand the test?'*

You can't get a much older friend than Scott. Not that he's ancient – he's the same age as me – what I mean is that we've been friends forever.

No one could possibly come between us.

'Science test today. Got your book?' Scott says as I get to the door.

I turn around, go back upstairs and rescue it from under a pile of magazines.

'And don't forget your umbrella – it looks like rain!' he adds as I come back down.

'Rain? *Nooo*, can my life get any worse!'

'Come on drama diva – it's just drizzle.'

'Yeah, but drizzle means frizzle and I've just done my hair! You know what happens when it gets wet – *hair-scare nightmare.*'

'Well, go get your brolly or we'll be late for school!'

'S'OK. It's in my bag. Last week's free gift from one of my magazines.'

'Well at least they've got some use,' Scott mutters as he shuts the front door and we set off to Westfield High.

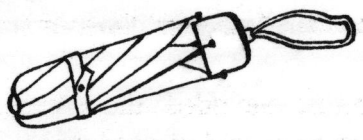

'So, did you revise last night?' Scott asks as we walk our usual route.

'Mmm well, I tried to but then I sort of got distracted by my new mag. I had to check out my stars...'

'Yeah, but that only takes two minutes! So what stopped you revising?'

'Oh, you know, then I glanced at one or two more pages...the *Top Ten Tips for a Dream-Date Diva* and the *True Confessions of a Psycho-Teen Killer* and the *Dish-The-Dirt Diary* of this girl who married her best friend's dog—'

'Maddy, why do you read that trash? What's the point?'

'It's not trash, Scott. It's REAL LIFE! I feel sorry for boys... How do you know what to try and what to buy, who's in and who's out, what's hot and what's not if you don't read mags?'

'And how do you know the Periodic Table, Newton's Third Law and the life cycle of a fruit fly if you don't study?'

'Oh, get real Scott. What's the use of knowing all that stuff? Um...you will sit next to me in the science test, won't you? And make sure you write in extra big letters, too.'

'Yes and I'll be your private surgeon when you need that brain implant in a few years' time. After all, what are friends for?'

'Ooh, you've just reminded me. Friends... Listen to this, Destiny Dreamer said there'd be a new person coming into my life. It's all to do with a star shooting into my planetary area...'

'Sounds painful,' Scott says, dragging me past a newsagent's before I can sneak a peek at the mags.

'Aww, come on Scott, just five minutes. Maybe this new person's in that shop right now and—'

'Or maybe the new person is the teacher on late duty today. You can get to know them better at lunchtime detention...but if that's not in your Cosmic Plan, keep walking and stop talking. Oh, and get your brolly out. It's frizz-alert time.'

'*Aaaagh!*' I manage to keep walking, screaming and scrabbling about in my bag at the same time. Finally I have to give up.

'Scott, stop!' I say, taking shelter from the rain in a doorway. 'Someone's stolen my umbrella – I'm sure I put it in my bag last night...or did I?'

He pauses briefly, whips out an umbrella and opens it. 'Let's go!'

But I can't move. My mouth has twisted into an extra-wide cover-girl smile.

'Scott? I don't *believe* it! Who would have guessed you were a brolly-dolly! And purple polka dots are so your style.'

'Don't push it, baby. Mum made me take it this morning. And no one argues with Nurse Hyacinth Lord on the warpath. Not that I need it, a bit of rain never hurt anyone...' He starts to close the umbrella again.

'*No, wait!*' I dodge under it and we huddle up as he opens it out again. '*Thankyou-thankyou-thankyou,* Scott. Where would I be without you?'

'Wet!'

We don't say much more till we get to school.

Scott's fast and focussed and I'm fat and breathless trotting at his side to keep up.

♥ ★ ♡

We reach the school gates just before the bell goes.

'You'd better ditch the purple hair-protector now,' I say, even though it's still raining. 'Don't want to ruin your image...'

This is the ultimate sacrifice – I'm still risking frizz-factor 8 (on a scale of 1–10) with the short walk across the school yard.

'It's cool,' Scott says. 'Let them laugh. We've come this far. Like I said, what are friends for?'

Typical Scott. Still looking out for me – he's done that ever since nursery. We met when he told this big kid to give my Barbie doll back. I stopped crying and made Scott laugh by getting Barbie to chat up his dumper truck.

At that time, my doll was my only friend. Since then it's been me and Scott against the world...

Other Orchard Books you might enjoy

Clarice Bean Spells Trouble	Lauren Child	978 1 84362 858 3*
The Truth Cookie	Fiona Dunbar	978 1 84362 549 0*
Cupid Cakes	Fiona Dunbar	978 1 84362 688 6
Chocolate Wishes	Fiona Dunbar	978 1 84362 689 3*
Clair de Lune	Cassandra Golds	978 1 84362 926 9
The Truth about Josie Green	Belinda Hollyer	978 1 84362 885 9
Hothouse Flower	Rose Impey	978 1 84616 215 2
My Scary Fairy Godmother	Rose Impey	978 1 84362 683 1
Shooting Star	Rose Impey	978 1 84362 560 5
Forever Family	Gill Lobel	978 1 84616 211 4*
Do Not Read – Or Else	Pat Moon	978 1 84616 082 0
Stargirl	Jerry Spinelli	978 1 84616 599 3* (pink cover) 978 1 84616 600 6* (silver cover)

All priced at £4.99 except those marked * which are £5.99

Orchard Red Apples are available from all good bookshops,
or can be ordered direct from the publisher:
Orchard Books, PO BOX 29, Douglas IM99 1BQ
Credit card orders please telephone 01624 836000
or fax 01624 837033
or visit our Internet site: www.wattspub.co.uk
or e-mail: bookshop@enterprise.net for details.

To order please quote title, author and ISBN
and your full name and address.
Cheques and postal orders should be made payable to 'Bookpost plc.'
Postage and packing is FREE within the UK
(overseas customers should add £1.00 per book).

Prices and availability are subject to change.